ELYSIUM

TONY HORAN

ISBN: 978-1-64184-681-3 (Paperback)
ISBN: 978-1-64184-682-0 (Ebook)

CONTENTS

PROLOGUE

Five thousand light years from the planet Earth, the most developed planet of the many universes in existence is the planet Elysium. Its inhabitants evolved into a race of beings far superior to those on Earth, both physically and mentally, and their lifespans often exceeded a thousand Earth years. Having developed the ability to travel faster than the speed of light several centuries ago, it took many more years of research into wormholes (structures linking disparate points in spacetime) before time and inter-universal travel became realities. With the ability to travel instantaneously to any of the trillions of planets in the billions of galaxies in each universe, Elysium rulers decided to assist suitable planets in developing their technological and humanitarian capabilities. Once planets achieved space travel capabilities and inhabitants were considered sufficiently mentally developed to accept the many different life forms in existence, they would be accepted into membership of the interplanetary federation. Their initial attempts to help worlds develop resulted in failures, and they soon realised that trying to provide the inhabitants with

Elysium technologies did not work. So, they decided to send a few Elysium scholars to planets with the purpose of integrating into the local communities and teaching them how to slowly develop their capabilities without interfering by providing them with technically advanced products which had failed in the past.

1

ELYSIUM, JANUARY 2015
EARTH TIME

Elysium's Divine Council, chaired by Atlas the current Chosen, were meeting in the Grand Hall. The eleven-member Council were comfortably seated, and apart from Atlas were wondering why this special meeting had been called. Atlas stood and regarded the Council members, selected after centuries of public service. The youngest member was just over five hundred years old, and except for the Chosen, the oldest member had recently celebrated his nine hundredth birthday. In addition to their educational achievements and physical fitness, members had to complete an extensive psychological assessment, be a minimum two hundred years old, and pass a mental and physical test every century.

Atlas addressed the current five male and five female members of the Council with a grave expression on his face. "It appears that once again we have a crisis in the worst problem planet in the countless planets we have settled over the past several thousand years. This meeting will consist of two parts – first to listen to a lengthy report from Traveller Azriel, and second to decide what steps, if any, the Council needs to take." As Atlas re-took his seat, Azriel entered the room and stood at a podium in front of the Council.

"Respected Council members, I would like to provide you with a brief background of our many centuries experience with planet three of a G2V (yellow dwarf) star in the Milky Way Galaxy, known as the planet Earth." "Shortly after my acceptance in the Traveller program, I was assigned to study the planet Earth before moving there permanently in their year 1960. Back then, Earth's population was around 3 billion humans after an estimated seven million years since the first human ancestors appeared. However, during my time there the population had more than doubled to 7 billion in 2015."

Azriel then went into a detailed explanation of how 100,000 years earlier, Elysium sent the standard twelve-person settlement team to Earth. The team's purpose was to follow Elysium's policy of integration with existing humanoid inhabitants to speed up the planet's development. The initial twelve settled in different areas of the planet although Earth's history books only contained limited details concerning Adam who was the leader of the original twelve. He married Eve, one of the Terrans, the original humanoid Earth inhabitants, and they had over twenty children before passing away. Adam lived for 930 years, slightly less than the average Elysian, but Eve lived to be well over 100 years old, far longer than the average Terran life expectancy at the time. It's possible that Adam's medical knowledge plus Elysian medication helped prolong her life. Over the ages, due to this inter-breeding between Elysians and Terrans, life spans slowly decreased from the Elysian 1,000-year average age. Terrans however saw a significant increase in their life expectancy from below 30 years to the current Earth average of 100 years.

As in most of the cultures we have experienced, religion was used as a method of controlling the population. On Earth the religions developed from worshipping the sun, trees, idols and multiple Gods to their current beliefs which for most inhabitants is one God. As Earth's population grew major problems occurred, and the Divine Council saw the need to place individual Elysians on Earth to prevent major catastrophes. So, the Traveller program developed with many more Elysians going to Earth than other planets. Earth was becoming an extremely warlike planet, and even the religions were unable to change that. Traveller 300, known as Moses, attempted uniting people, and provided them with something he called the Ten Commandments to promote a general guide on how people should live their lives. However, it wasn't until Traveller 350, Jesus Christ, that significant steps in creating an ordered society were made. The Earth's most used calendar, which I'm using for the purpose of this presentation, starts with the year Jesus first went to the Earth. Jesus was treated very badly by several of the existing religious groups, in particular the Jewish leaders who alleged he was guilty of many crimes including blasphemy. They convinced the Roman leaders to sentence him to death, and we had to bring him back to Elysium before he could complete his work. His followers were called Christians, and he taught them that God although one entity was also a trinity of God the Father, God the Son being Jesus, and God the Holy Spirit who united the Christians with Christ. The main themes Jesus taught were: Love – God, your neighbour, your enemies; Forgive – others who have wronged you, ask God to forgive your sins; Don't – be hypocritical, judge others. He had trained several competent assistants who managed to spread his teachings and Earth was slowly developing in the right direction. From a very small group of people, by 2015 there were 2.4 billion Christians, making Christianity the largest religion for over 31% of Earth's population.

Some five hundred years after he was recalled, one of the Terrans, Mohamed, attempted to recreate the work Jesus started and ended up creating a new religion called Islam. They also have their own calendar, the Hijri calendar, which started the year Mohamed migrated from the city of Makkah to the city of Medina in the Christian calendar year 622. Although both calendars contain 12 months, the Hijri calendar has fewer days in their month. Their Holy book, The Koran, called for the spread of the religion and Mohamed and his followers were very successful in converting people to the religion he called Islam, and killed or enslaved those who refused to convert. Their adherents, called Muslims, numbered over 1.9 billion in 2015, making them the second largest religion followed by nearly 25% of the population. There are also an estimated 1.2 billion non-religious people and several other religions of which the largest are Hinduism and Buddhism. Mohammed was an extremely intelligent man, and he used Islam to correct a lot of problems with his converts. Having them pray five times a day, he got them to perform ablutions before prayer which was a great change from them not washing very often. He also made pigs Haram in the Koran as many people were getting sick from eating pork which doesn't keep very long in their hot climate. In addition, he increased the punishment for crimes, and in a master stroke he introduced the death penalty for anyone criticizing Islam. The core beliefs of Islam, called the Five Pillars of Islam, are Profession of Faith, Prayer, Alms, Fasting, and performing a pilgrimage to Mecca also called the Hajj.

Although the various religions lived in harmony some time, several centuries after Mohamed, the Christians attacked Muslims in the Middle East in a series of religious wars started primarily to take control of holy sites both groups considered sacred. A few centuries later another warring group called Mongols continued the Christian attacks and the Islamic civilization suffered terribly. The centre of the Islamic Empire was Baghdad which was besieged and captured by the Mongols in 1258, an event considered one of the most catastrophic events in the history of Islam. Even today Islam has two main groups, Sunnis and Shiites with their main difference being political leadership. The largest group, Sunnis, believe that Mohammed's successor should be a pious individual who followed Mohammed's customs, whereas the Shiites felt Mohammed's successor should be someone in his bloodline.

All religions strive to promote peace and harmony, but there remain fanatics who believe in the superiority of their own religion and try to impose their version of truth upon others.

In the latter half of the 18th century, Earth had a period of development called the Industrial Revolution which transformed largely rural, agrarian societies into industrial, urban ones. The 19th century and early 20th centuries saw a second period of industrialization with rapid advancements in many industries. Demand for energy increased substantially, and following the use of coal, oil and natural gas were used to fill the demands initially. Several countries continued to battle against each other, and there were two major world wars, the second one ending shortly after the discovery of nuclear power. World War II started when Germany invaded Poland, and the main participants were the "Axis" powers (Germany, Italy and Japan), and the "Allies" (France, Great Britain, The United States of America and Russia). The war lasted six years and claimed the lives of an estimated 80 million people or approximately 3% of the World's population. The final surrender came after the United States dropped two nuclear bombs on Japan

One of the biggest impacts on the planet from the demand for oil was to create extremely wealthy countries, many of which were Islamic. These countries started investing heavily in non-Islamic counties and played a major role in spreading Islam to these so-called Western countries. With the second World War revealing the terrible devastation caused by nuclear power, the major Western countries stockpiled nuclear weapons as a deterrent to other countries using them again. Islamic countries are continually trying to develop the technology, and one of the West's major fears is an Islamic nuclear attack due to the Islamic terrorists' disregard for human life other than their own religion followers. Even they are considered acceptable deaths in the destruction of the Great Satan they call non-Muslims. Significant amounts of cash have been funnelled to hard-line Islamic extremists and they are currently negotiating with former Western military groups to purchase nuclear weapons. Although the major powers agree that a nuclear war would devastate the planet and should be avoided at all costs, there is a growing concern that terrorists would not consider the implications of a nuclear holocaust. Having committed several terrorist atrocities including murdering some 3,000 people in New York, a major city in the United States of America, on what is called the September 11 attacks, it seems that fanatics from the Wahhabi terrorist group Al-Qaeda are the most likely group to attempt nuclear attacks. Their founder, Osama bin Laden, was from Saudi Arabia although the group operates in several countries in the Middle East and North Africa.

There are currently nine countries in possession of nuclear weapons, Russia (formerly The Soviet Union), the United States, China, India, Israel, France, North Korea, Pakistan, and the United Kingdom. However, when the Soviet Union collapsed in 1991, three newly independent states, Belarus, Kazakhstan and Ukraine, had an estimated 3,200 strategic nuclear weapons that were deactivated and returned to Russia. There is widespread belief that not all the nuclear weapons were returned. After giving the Council the brief history of Earth's more recent major events, Azriel continued his talk.

"During my time on Earth, I was intrigued to learn about an individual called Jason Steele. I read an article written by a Doctor Macintosh in 'The Lancet', one of their medical journals, about Jason which caused me to investigate him more thoroughly. I contacted Doctor Mackintosh who still retained a sample of Jason Steel's blood. Using some of this blood, I was able to examine his DNA and found it contained a large amount of DNA of Elysium origin. Over the centuries Elysians have developed electrocyte cells that protect us against electric shocks and Jason Steele also had these cells. Researching him further I could find no mention of him before 2009 but I did find out the first record of him was a flight from New York to London which occurred a few weeks after Stephen Bailey, an American inventor and physicist, was executed in New York by a device called the electric chair. He had been found guilty of murdering his wife and daughter, although he strongly denied his guilt up to the time of his execution. It appears that Stephen survived the electrical current, which affected his cells, and he is slowly mutating into a being with Elysian physical characteristics. He changed his name to Jason Steele and devoted his time to discovering who had murdered his family.

His investigations led him to Saudi Arabia where he discovered why his wife and daughter were murdered and who committed the crime. He had been in the process of developing a powerful miniature battery that would virtually eliminate the demand for fossil fuels, which make up some 90% of the Saudi economy. To prevent Stephen from completing the battery, one of the Saudi's working for an influential Prince came up with the complex plan to incriminate Stephen for the murders and have him either imprisoned for life or executed.

After considering the impact his battery would have on oil producing countries, Stephen, now Jason, managed to get a job working for the Saudi company responsible for oil production. During a field trip searching for oil, his group were attacked by fanatics and Makram, the Saudi in charge of the trip, was fatally wounded by the terrorists. Before dying, he told Jason that when he arrived in Saudi, he had immediately recognised him as being Stephen Bailey, and that he was responsible for murdering Stephen's family in New York. He greatly regretted his actions and was overjoyed to see that Stephen had somehow survived. A few members of Jason's party overheard the death bed confession and offered to accompany Jason back to the USA to clear his name. However, having achieved his goal of finding out who murdered his family, Jason left Saudi and after getting married in England to a woman he met in Saudi, is now living in London.

Although we have never revealed our origins to Terrans, I am approaching the Divine Council to request their permission for me to attempt recruiting Jason Steele to head off the nuclear holocaust we think is a distinct possibility. In addition to being a leading physicist, he is fluent in Arabic and is slowly developing

Elysian capabilities. To recruit Jason, I would like to bring him and his wife Anita to Elysium where we can expedite his transformation as well as subjecting Anita to molecular transformation to make her life span and physical attributes consistent with her husbands. In addition to his experience in Saudi Arabia and the oil industry, I think the terrorists will probably be from the Middle East making his fluent Arabic capabilities essential. Although I do not want to put pressure on the Council, we do not have a lot of time if we are to prevent the potential destruction of the planet. It did not take the Divine Council very long to agree with Azriel, even though it technically went against their rules of non-intervention in a planet's evolution. Failure to act would eliminate billions of people and leave a planet that would be uninhabitable for centuries.

2

ORINDA CALIFORNIA, NOVEMBER 2009

It was another glorious summer's day in Orinda with a vivid blue cloudless sky and a temperature of 80 degrees Fahrenheit. David Bailey was enjoying his Sunday and had just finished working on his flower garden. It was almost nine months since his only son, Steve, had been executed and he'd inherited the beautiful Orinda home. Although Steve's murdered wife Paula had left all her possessions to her parents, they wanted nothing to do with Steve or his family and turned down David's offer to take whatever they wanted from the family home. The large five bedroomed property in Orinda was far too big for David on his own, but he stayed living there for sentimental reasons. Following the unbelievable news that Steve survived the execution and had taken the identity of a former childhood friend, Jason Steele, David agreed to run Steve's Mercury Corporation until he retired as CEO last year. He still travelled to the head office in San Francisco each weekday although his guidance was needed less and less by his more than adequate replacement. The company was still producing the gas engine that turned them into a billion-dollar corporation, and David was still the 51% owner from Steve's will

Prior to Steve's incarceration, he had been working on a miniature battery that would revolutionise the car industry. Unfortunately, the project had to be shelved as they were unable to find a scientist able to finish Steve's work. David was concerned that demand for the Stirling gas engine would be greatly reduced once a practical miniature battery was developed and was hoping for the day that Steve would return to a more normal life and continue developing his battery.

The telephone interrupted David's reminiscing and he walked into the kitchen to answer it. "Hi dad, It's Jason" his son said. "I hope I'm not interrupting you, but I have a few very important items to discuss with you." After reassuring Jason that he had just finished gardening and was simply taking a rest, Jason continued "I've met a young widowed English woman in Saudi, and I am planning on marrying her. I realize it's going to be a big surprise, but we have so much in common and I know she is going to give me a purpose in life again. We are leaving Saudi next month, and as soon as the wedding plans are finalised, I would like you to come to England where we will be married." "I'm so happy for you Jason, and you know I would never miss your wedding" replied David. "What will you do in England after the marriage? It would be great if you could return to California and finish your battery project." "Sorry dad but that isn't on the cards in the near future. I'm still a little concerned about returning to the USA after my court case, even though I have a pretty fool proof new identity.

In addition, during my stay in Saudi I was on a desert trip when my boss, Makram, was murdered." "Oh my goodness," said David, "Makram was one of my contacts in Saudi. I rescued him from being attacked by wild dogs when he was a young boy living in Libya. He really helped my career with his influential father but had to leave Libya after the 1969 revolution there." Jason was shocked to hear Makram was one of David's friends. "I'm not sure if he knew you were my father, but before he died Makram admitted murdering Paula and Anita in an attempt to halt the development of my battery project. He did that under the direction of some of the Saudi Royal family and I know there is no way I could ever get them in a court room. His admission was witnessed by a couple of people who said they would come to the USA and clear my name. However, as they both worked for me, I'm not sure how well their testimony would be received in the USA. It's quite a coincidence that my fiancé is also called Anita. I want to live for a while in surroundings she is familiar with. Her husband was murdered in front of her very recently, and although we have a great relationship, I want to take things slowly with our new life together." David thought that if Makram knew Jason was his son he would never have carried out the murders. Although he was anxious for Jason to restart his battery design, he appreciated his concerns over Anita and said his goodbyes.

3

DHAHRAN, JANUARY 2010

The moving company had packed the few items Jason and Anita wanted shipped to the UK, and the shipment would be held at a storage facility near Manchester Airport for three months until they had a permanent address. Their last night in Dhahran was spent in the guest house at the Saudi National Oil Company (SOCO) compound. A going away party had been arranged for them, and they were very glad to be booked on a late afternoon flight the following day. Mike Williams, the SOCO Human Resources Manager, spoke to the guests and said how sorry they were to see Jason leave after spending only a year with SOCO. However, he added, I am pleased to announce that Jason has agreed to taking a consultancy agreement with us so we will probably see him back here in the not too distant future. Jason thanked Mike, and said he regretted leaving Saudi so soon, but he had urgent personal business to take care of in the UK which gave him no option but to resign.

He explained later to his friend John Nash that he didn't think it appropriate to marry Anita in Saudi Arabia, and the real reason for his resignation was to marry Anita as soon as possible in the UK. John was surprised to hear there were wedding plans so soon for the couple. Anita had been widowed a few months earlier, when her husband, Sabah, was murdered by an Islamic terrorist. John congratulated Jason and admitted that he would have been first in the line of Anita's suitors if Jason hadn't been so fortunate to form an apparently permanent relationship with her. Jason said he would still like John to be his best man when he got married and John laughed and said no problem with that. It was obvious to me for a long time that Anita had eyes for you and no one else.

Although Jason was giving away a lot of his clothes and planned to leave with just one suitcase, Anita had several possessions she wanted to take with her on the flight as well as a fair amount of clothing, so they would be leaving Saudi with several suitcases. Jason was leaving his collection of alcohol to John, and asked John to take them to the airport in his large Suburban. The journey from Dhahran to Dammam took about 30 minutes along the Dhahran to Jubail Expressway and after they said goodbye to John, they joined the small line at the First-Class check in. The Etihad airlines flight from Dammam to Manchester was almost full, but Jason and Anita had plenty of space in their first-class seats. When the steward asked them what would they like to drink before take-off, he apologised and explained they were unable to serve alcohol until the flight was airborne, but they had some very nice

Bollinger champagne available in the air. Jason and Anita both had orange juice and relaxed in their sleeper seats for twenty minutes before take-off. The flight wasn't direct, having a stopover in Abu Dhabi which was about one hour's flying time from Dammam, but all passengers for Manchester had to remain on the plane in Abu Dhabi while some passengers deplaned, and others came on board.

On leaving Dammam, and as soon as the seatbelt sign was off, some of the Saudi women went to the rest rooms dressed in their abayas and exited in modern Western clothing. When Jason passed a comment about this transformation, Anita explained that many of the younger Western educated Saudi ladies preferred the Western style clothing but had to wear their abayas in Saudi to prevent their fathers or husbands getting into trouble with the Muttawa, Saudi's religious police. Jason reflected on how lucky he had been to be brought up in America where men and women were equal in the eyes of the law. Western women had to fight for many years to get their equality, but could now enjoy being able to vote and drive, unlike their Saudi counterparts. He was still amazed that after so many of their senior citizens were receiving Western education, they still followed such discriminatory treatment of women who were unable to travel freely like their male counterparts and even inherited half the amount a male sibling would receive. Anita had many talks with Sabah before they were married, and he explained that even though he was a Muslim he didn't agree with all the restrictions being placed on women and that there were calls for change in Saudi. He thought women would be driving within the next ten years and said that Saudi was better than some countries where the men did not want girls to receive an education and actually attacked schools that ignored them.

Relaxing in their seats enjoying their glasses of champagne, Jason asked Anita if she was certain that Manchester was the place she wanted to settle down in after their wedding. He explained how his father successfully ran the family business in San Francisco until last year and still attended the company's board meetings being a 51% owner. The company is valued in the billions and provides far more money than they would ever need to live comfortably, so he was free to settle wherever she wanted. Anita's parents lived in Bramhall, a suburban area of Greater Manchester, and Anita told Jason that she would like to stay with her parents for a few weeks while the wedding arrangements were made, have an exotic honeymoon, and then decide on where to make their home. Jason agreed, and after their very enjoyable dinner once the plane left Abu Dhabi, extended their sleeper seats and fell asleep. They were woken up when the pilot announced they would be landing in 40 minutes and to expect snow and a 37 degrees Fahrenheit arrival temperature. Anita was secretly worried that her parents may be unhappy about her relationship with Jason so soon after Sabah's murder, but hoped that on meeting Jason they would be as taken by him as she was.

4

MANCHESTER AIRPORT, JANUARY 2010

With a very smooth landing, the plane touched down just before 10am in softly falling snow and a thirty-seven-degree temperature. The pilot told passengers there would be a slight delay in leaving the aircraft caused by a technical problem with the passenger boarding bridge that should be resolved very quickly. As the plane was twenty minutes ahead of schedule, there would not be a problem for any passengers with connecting flights.

Jason and Anita soon exited the plane, and once they cleared immigration headed to baggage collection where they had several suitcases to collect. Hiring a porter to help with their baggage, they walked through the nothing to declare line without a problem. They did recognise one very overweight English gentleman from their flight whose two suitcases had been selected for a search and appeared to contain nothing but cartons of cigarettes. Their porter explained this was becoming a common problem with passengers from Saudi, as cigarettes could be purchased in Saudi at a fraction of the UK cost. Although the cigarettes would be confiscated if found, some people risked getting them through customs illegally as they would be able to sell them in the UK making enough money to pay for their holidays. They were amazed that people who were already making very good tax-free salaries in Saudi as well as having accommodation and in some cases even food provided would take such risks in smuggling cigarettes. On asking the porter what would happen to the passenger, he answered that to the best of his knowledge the cigarettes would be seized, and the passenger's name would be flagged, so he would definitely be checked the next time he came into the country. Jason was surprised that a smuggler would not be at least fined for breaking the law but assumed that if it was a first offence he may have got away with a warning.

It was only six miles from the airport to Anita's parents' home in Bramhall. Because of the bad weather, Jason had asked Anita to tell her parents they would make their own way to their house as he didn't want them to drive to the airport after checking the weather forecast before leaving Saudi. The airport was fairly busy, so Jason decided to hire a limousine to take them to Bramhall. On leaving the terminal building they were rudely reminded of the temperature difference from the seventy degrees in Dammam at their departure. It was Jason's first trip to the Manchester area, and after a few miles on a dual carriageway the car turned on to a single carriageway and Jason saw signs for villages like Styall and Cheadle Hulme before reaching Bramhall. Anita pointed out Cheadle Hulme School and told Jason that was her Grammar school before she went on to Manchester University. Founded in 1855 and originally called Manchester's Warehousemen and Clerks' Orphan School, by the time Anita went there in 1992 it was called Cheadle Hulme School and had more than 1,000 pupils. Anita's father, Peter Smith, had been educated at the same school. When he went there in 1957 it was a fee-paying school with a large proportion of boarders. Peter passed his 11 plus examination with such high results he was offered a free place at the school. One of his childhood friends also passed the 11 plus but only qualified for a regular Grammar School. However, his parents, who could luckily afford it, agreed to pay the annual fees so their son could continue to enjoy is friendship with Peter. Another of her father's friends also won a free scholarship, and her father was his best man when he got married in 1969. They still remain friends after all these years and meet up a few times a year to go hiking and even walking up mountains together. Their last big mountain was Ben Nevis which they walked up last July before getting to their 60th birthdays.

Arriving at Anita's parents' home in Manor Close, Bramhall, Jason was impressed by the spacious 3,000 square foot building. Although the upstairs had four bedrooms, one en-suite bathroom, and a separate family bathroom, the downstairs area was twice as large as the upstairs. It had a large open plan family/kitchen/dining area, a sitting room, formal lounge, office, utility room, shower room and a double garage. There was a large driveway, extensive gardens and the property overlooked the Bramhall Park golf course. Anita's parents, Peter and Mavis, lived alone in the house, as Anita's only sister, Helen, was married to Richard and lived near Bournemouth in Dorset. With both girls having left home and not having grandchildren, they had often talked about downsizing at some time in the future. So, Jason and Anita's visit made a pleasant change to their quiet lifestyle.

Peter and Jane welcomed the couple, and Jane asked Peter to give Jason a tour of the house while she and Anita made a pot of tea. Jason's first impressions of Anita's parents was positive, being readily accepted by them into their home. Peter was well built, still handsome and must be playing some sport in addition to his hiking to appear so athletic. The similarity between Mavis and Anita was remarkable, and it was obvious to Jason that Anita had inherited her mother's good looks. Following the tour, Jason refused Peter's offer to help take their suitcases to the guest bedroom saying I'm sure you and Jane would rather spend a little time with Anita, and I'll join you in a few minutes. With his recently acquired strength, Jason had little difficulty in finishing the job far faster than Peter believed possible.

As they had both been able to sleep on the flight to Manchester, Anita suggested having lunch at the Hesketh Arms, a local pub, then driving on a little further to look at Peter's old church, St. Andrew's, in Cheadle Hulme. Although small, Anita thought it was ideal for their wedding location and just a few doors away from Peter's childhood home on Cheadle Road which was still in the family as a rental property.

Following university, Peter joined an architectural company and finally made partner giving him a very comfortable lifestyle.

The Hesketh Arms was close to Anita's old school and just a few doors away from the sweet shop so many students frequented over the years. Jason remembered Anita telling him how her industrious father as a new eleven-year-old student used to buy liquorice at the shop and sell it to his classmates for twice its cost. He had been impressed at how Peter had been such a hard-working child who in addition to working as a paperboy in the mornings and evenings, helped the shop owner in marking the papers for the several paperboys as well as serving in the shop at the weekends.

Following a very enjoyable lunch that Jason paid for before Peter realised what was happening, they all went to the Vicarage opposite St. Andrews church. The vicar, Dick Sergeant, welcomed Peter even though he hadn't been to church for many years. Peter introduced his daughter Anita and her fiancé Jason, and said they were getting married and would like the wedding to take place in St. Andrews. The vicar explained to Jason and Anita that 28 days' notice must be given to the Register Office before a marriage could take place in England and Wales. It also required the couple to be resident for seven days in England or Wales before notice is given. The notice must also state where the marriage is to take place. Agreeing to all the conditions including having the wedding banns (notice of the proposed marriage) read in the church for three Sundays before the ceremony, a wedding date was set for Saturday, February 27. Anita was given the task of sending out the wedding invitations and Jason said his only invitees would be his father, David Bailey, and his former work colleague John Nash who he would like as his best man.

Returning home, Peter insisted that Jason and Anita stay with them until after the wedding which was gratefully accepted. Discussing their immediate future, Jason decided to apply for a teaching position in the Physics department at Manchester University. Although he already had a consultancy agreement with his former employer, the Saudi National Oil Company (SOCO), he knew he would be completely bored if that was his only work. Being a member of the Physics department would provide an avenue for training future scientists as well as allowing him to perform research in areas concerning the miniaturization of batteries. With Jason's wholehearted blessings, Anita decided to enrol in a master's degree in Geoscience, a topic she became really interested in after working for Jason in Saudi Arabia.

Jason was fortunate in his teaching application. One of the Physics professors was taking early retirement and based on his qualifications being verified, Jason was an ideal candidate. If he could attend an interview process as soon as possible, the University was certain there would be a position for him. They agreed for the interview to take place the following Tuesday. Anita wanted to take Jason on a tour of the places in Bramhall she really loved in her youth. Luckily as the weekend weather was dry although cold, she was able to show Jason most of her childhood haunts. They started off at Bramhall Hall, a Tudor Manor House with origins back to the Middle Ages. Anita took Jason for a short walk in the woodlands and explained there were around 70 acres of parkland and that when they had more time, they had to do a tour of the Hall itself. After some four hours of seeing Anita's favourite spots, they ended up in the Ladybrook pub for lunch. It was a very large place and Anita said it was a hotel before but had been one of her favourite pubs when she was living there. It was a mile away from Peter and Mavis's home and had been very good for a place to have a drink and not worry about driving. Lunch was very enjoyable and reasonably priced, and the happy couple took a leisurely walk back home.

Anita decided to have a shopping day in Manchester while Jason had his interview, which went very quickly. He was interviewed by three professors who asked fairly straightforward questions and were more than satisfied by Jason's responses. Being asked when he would be available, Jason answered that he was getting married on February 27, and would be available three weeks later. The university agreed on the start date, salary and promised to send an offer letter as soon as possible. Jason thanked the interviewers and said he was really looking forward to being on the staff of such an impressive University. Meeting up with Anita at the Arndale Centre in Manchester, Jason gave her the good news about the job and said they agreed on him starting after their honeymoon, so everything was falling into place. Anita congratulated Jason and asked if it would be OK for her to continue shopping as the interview took far less time than she expected. They both picked up some new clothing for the honeymoon and returned home with several full shopping bags.

5

CHEADLE HULME,
FEBRUARY 2010

Although it was cold, the wintry sun provided dancing warm rays shining through the clouds onto the church as Anita arrived with her father in their rented Rolls Royce Silver Shadow. Jason was already standing by the altar at the front of the church next to John Nash as Peter walked down the aisle with Anita on his arm. David Bailey, Jason's father, was standing in the right front pew with a few of his colleagues from San Francisco. Mavis and several of her friends were standing in the left pews as all turned to watch Anita walk down the aisle. Anita looked stunning in her Oscar de la Renta wedding dress selected after many hours of searching with Mavis for the perfect dress for her daughter's second wedding. A tear came to Mavis's eye as she saw how handsome Peter looked in the same Windsor Tuxedo that he wore for the first time at Anita's first wedding, but which still fit him like a glove. In no time at all the wedding ceremony was over and the wedding party headed to the reception at the Lancaster Suite in Manchester's Midland Hotel.

The Midland Hotel has been one of Manchester's preferred hotels for over one hundred years and is in the centre of town. In addition to valet parking, the hotel is close to St. Peter's Square tram stop and many of the attendees were using public transport. After a drink's reception in the Chester Suite, the party moved into the Derby Suite where an elaborate meal was served followed by dancing until the early hours. Peter had booked the newly weds into the Midland suite for the night and they took an early exit from the wedding party as Peter explained they had a flight at noon the following day to Thailand where they were starting their honeymoon. Feeling a little tired after the hectic day and not relishing their wake-up call, the couple still enjoyed cuddling each other which led to mind blowing sex before they finally fell asleep.

Their 7 am wake-up call came far too soon, and after a mad dash to get ready, they caught their limousine getting to the airport in plenty of time for their British Airways flight to Bangkok via London. With just over a one-hour layover in London, their flight to Bangkok left at 13:50 and arrived in Bangkok the following morning at 9:45. Mavis had taken charge of Anita's wedding dress and Peter did the same with Jason's tuxedo, so the couple only had one suitcase each to be checked in.

6

FAR EAST, FEBRUARY 2010

Touching down at Bangkok's Suvarnabhumi Airport, Jason and Anita received VIP treatment from the first hotel on their honeymoon, the Peninsula Hotel in Bangkok. After clearing immigration and customs, they were escorted to one of the hotel's Green Rolls Royce Silver Clouds and whisked away to the hotel which is located on the banks of Bangkok's major river, the majestic Chao Phraya. They had both enjoyed long sleeps during the 16-hour flight, again made possible by their business class seats. Although Jason could easily afford First Class tickets, he was more than happy with the comfort and service in business class. Having used British Airways on several business class flights to Saudi, Jason had already earned a Gold Executive Club card which allowed him to use the First-Class airport lounges in addition to other benefits.

The hotel has a complimentary boat that lets you out at the Thaksin sky train stop, and although crowded, the sky train is the fastest way to get around Bangkok. The next few days were spent doing the hotel's recommended tourist attractions including the Grand Palace, a river cruise, the floating market and many of the beautiful and intricate temples Thailand has to offer. Anita was particularly impressed with their visits to the MBK Center and the Siam Paragon, where she found it hard to believe how many different types of store were so close to each other. While the MBK Center appeared to have knock-off clothes and electronics, the Siam Paragon contained designer clothes and upscale shopping at correspondingly higher prices.

The one drawback to Bangkok was the amount of traffic, which made it difficult to get round to the many places they would have liked to visit but were a long way from a sky train stop. Instead of a full day's sightseeing, they enjoyed lazing by the hotel pool with its views over the river in the afternoons. The food and drinks at the pool bar were pricey but excellent, and the pool area was like a beautiful tropical garden.

They found the Thai people very helpful and hardworking, and if you smiled at them, they returned the warmest friendly smile imaginable. Although there were many other places of interest in Thailand, they had decided beforehand to take this opportunity to visit several countries in the Far East on this trip. There would be plenty of time later to revisit places they liked the most. However, a cable handed to Jason on their last day in Thailand resulted in a quick change of plans. Professor George Clarkson, the American scientist in charge of the Manchester University Physics department, asked for Jason to report to the university two weeks earlier than planned. It was planned for Jason to replace a retiring general Physics lecturer, but since the professor responsible for the Universities courses in advanced electricity and magnetism was leaving the university to emigrate to Australia, they would really like Jason to fill the vacancy. Jason apologised to Anita over the need to cut their honeymoon short and explained they would still be able to visit Singapore, but would have to leave Vietnam, Korea and Japan to future adventures.

Singapore was just under a 3-hour plane ride away from Thailand. Following an uneventful flight from Bangkok, they landed at Changi Airport in Singapore in the early evening. Jason had prebooked a limousine to take them from the airport to the Marina Bay Sands hotel where they had the honeymoon suite booked for five days. The hotel had caught their attention after watching a half hour TV program on the hotel and its many amenities a week before the wedding. The hotel has the world's largest rooftop infinity pool on the 57th floor, and the couple took a lazy lunch at the poolside on their first day. They noted the marked difference in cleanliness after Bangkok and were looking forward to their afternoon guided tour of the City. Their first stop included the cultural districts of Chinatown, Little India and Arab Street. After visiting Singapore's Civic district, they ended up at the Raffles Hotel. Peter told them not to miss the Raffles Long Bar, so they each had a Singapore Sling in the bar where the floor was covered with peanut shells. Deciding to keep their glasses as a souvenir, the two drinks were definitely the most expensive on the trip so far.

Returning to their hotel, they changed for dinner and headed to the hotels' Lavo Italian restaurant which was situated on the rooftop and offered spectacular views over the city. After another amazing meal with friendly staff and excellent service, they retired to their suite to prepare for their following day's adventure. Jason had chartered a boat to take them from the West Coast Pier to Palau Hantu Island and to bring them back after their day of scuba diving and relaxing by the beach. The pair enjoyed their diving in the crystal-clear waters and were amazed at the variety of sea life they saw which included clownfish, angelfish, sea horses and even a giant clam.

Following a few more days exploring Singapore, they took a Singapore Airlines flight to London. This time Jason had booked First Class tickets for the 14-hour flight as he wanted to experience the Double Suites in Singapore Airlines Airbus A380. Checking in at Changi airport, they were directed to the luxurious check-in lounge for First Class and Suites passengers. Flying in the Suites also included an invitation to the "Private Room", which they reached after passing through the Business and First-Class lounges. "Good evening Mr. and Mrs. Steele" greeted the attractive receptionist, "and welcome to the Private Room. You are welcome to join us in our dining room or if you prefer just a drink in the lounge area." Not feeling hungry but interested in the menu, the couple walked to the dining area. The extensive menu included a Chicken and Mutton Satay plate, Baked Boston

Lobster, and a US Prime Beef Burger with Foie Gras, Rocket Leaf and Fried Quail Egg. Returning to the lounge, the couple settled for glasses of Dom Perignon champagne.

Walking to the dedicated Suites Class jet bridge, a flight attendant greeted them "Good evening Mr. & Mrs. Steele" She then escorted them to their double suite and offered another glass of Dom Perignon which was gratefully accepted. The flight departed at midnight and as soon as the safety belt signs were extinguished, James the Chief Steward offered more drinks but this time they ordered two of the Jamaican Blue Mountain coffees. James then said as they were the only passengers in the 12 Suites, they could have our bedroom, plus a dining room and a living room if they wanted. The meal service was declined, and James with a stewardess went about making up the double bed. On changing into the provided pyjamas in the rest room, the couple settled into the spacious double bed for the rest of the flight. They did wake up around 8 am and James was on hand to provide them with a full English breakfast. A few hours before arrival they both took advantage of the shower room and arrived in London completely refreshed. To soften the blow of the cut short honeymoon, Jason had booked a two day stay at the Savoy in London and took Anita to see the stage production of Evita as although she loved the music, she had never seen the stage show. Anita was captivated by the show and said they would have to bring her parents to see it as her mother would absolutely love both the acting and the incredible music. The hotel was fairly close to the theatre and they enjoyed a leisurely stroll back through streets full of theatre goers. Their hotel was definitely one of the better they had stayed in, and Anita was impressed by their suite which included their own dedicated butler service.

7
MANCHESTER, MARCH 2010

ollowing their incredible honeymoon in Thailand and Singapore, the couple arrived back after their hour-long flight from London to a cold day in Manchester. Before leaving on the trip, Jason had rented a fully furnished four-bedroom house on Abcomb Street which was within walking distance of Manchester University. The taxi from the airport dropped them off at the terraced house for which the rental agency had provided keys before their trip. Entering the house, they were impressed by its cleanliness although the furniture was relatively low cost. This was a little disappointing considering the hefty rental price of STG£ 1,750 per month. In addition to the four bedrooms and two bathrooms upstairs, there was a fully fitted dining room kitchen area, a spacious lounge with leather furniture and a small but tidy garden to the rear. Jason was pleased to see the rental agency had supplied them with the requested new soft furnishings including towels, bedding, cutlery etc he had specified from Anita's favourite Laura Ashley catalogue and paid for in advance. In walking distance from the house there was also a Spar convenience store on Oxford Street, and several restaurants, many of them American chains including Applebee's and TGI Fridays.

After settling into their new home and visiting Peter and Mavis over the weekend, Jason started his first day working in the University. The first class was on electricity and he was surprised by the lack of students for the class. The large lecture hall seemed virtually empty with only eight students, of which only one was female. Jason addressed the students and said "Good morning lady and gentlemen. My name is Doctor Jason Steele, but I would prefer you to call me Jason. I apologise for joining you after the start of the term, but your previous lecturer, Professor Andrew Moore, had to return to the USA, and I am very happy to take his place. I would like each of you to tell me your name, where you are from, and what you expect to get from this course." The students introduced themselves without incident until he came to one person who appeared to be a slightly older member of the class. Jason received a flash into his mind of "Could he be the one?" Jason had been able to subdue all the thoughts he'd been getting from people since his attempted execution and wondered why this thought had been able to get though. "My name is Mohamed Al-Sabah and I was born in Dhahran, Saudi Araba. I've enrolled in this course to increase my knowledge of electricity. My goal is to develop a smaller more effective battery which I believe will be the future for the automotive industry. I am also studying nuclear physics as power is a major issue in Saudi Arabia and although we have more than sufficient oil reserves at the moment, we need to research alternative sources for when our reserves are depleted".

Mohamed was very curious about Doctor Jason Steele. Jason was a popular first name in the West, as was the surname Steele. However, it was quite a coincidence that it was also the name of the person who murdered his favourite elder brother, Sabah. Although they had the same father, Mohamed's mother, Nadia, was her husband Ibrahim's youngest wife and had been brought up in a very religious family. Sabah was eleven years older and had treated him almost as a father would treat a son. Sabah had left Saudi to study in Great Britain when Mohamed was only six years old and he was deeply upset to lose the older brother he was so attached to. His mother was also upset that her stepson was leaving Saudi as she considered the West to be decadent and her parents had warned her about the evil people living there. She argued with her husband for months about Sabah leaving them but couldn't change his mind. So, she decided to send Mohamed to Riyadh to live with her father's younger brother Khalifa and his family. Khalifa was even more religious than her father and would ensure Mohamed would not have to face being indoctrinated by the West. Sabah continued to visit Saudi each year, and although he spent most of his time in Dhahran, he always took the time to visit Mohamed in Riyadh.

Ibrahim enrolled Sabah in a technical college in Manchester, where he developed an interest in Physics.

Following five years studying English and gaining three A levels in Maths, Physics and Chemistry, Sabah was accepted in Manchester University at the age of twenty-two for their undergraduate course in Physics. The four-year course was difficult, but he passed with honours and was accepted to the two-year graduate course. He finally graduated from Manchester University with an MSc in Physics when he was twenty-eight.

During his study in Manchester, he became infatuated with a local girl and following graduation took a position with Shell Oil Company in Altrincham, a town 8 miles from Manchester. Ibrahim wanted him to return to Saudi and take a job with SOCO, the Saudi Oil Company, but Sabah knew his father would try to get him to enter into an arranged marriage. Being single at twenty eight was unusual for a Saudi male, and there was talk of laws prohibiting a Saudi male from marrying a non-Saudi woman unless he was aged between 40 and 65. Sabah wrote to his father and told him that he had fallen in love with an English girl he intended to marry. On receiving the letter, a very irate Ibrahim telephoned him and made it clear the family would have nothing to do with him in the future if he didn't return to Saudi immediately and marry the very attractive girl they had picked for him.

Sabah disobeyed his father's orders and married the English student he met whilst at University. His wife, Anita Smith, had surprised her parents by being admitted to Manchester University at the age of 16. She also studied Physics and graduated with a BSc in Physics the same year as Sabah, after finishing the four-year course in just three years. One month after graduation the couple were married in Bramhall, and Anita's parents were happy to welcome Sabah into the family. There were no guests from Saudi at the wedding although Sabah had invited his parents and two of his many siblings.

Sabah spent the next three years working in Altrincham without a trip back to Saudi, but finally reconciled with his family and returned to live in Saudi. Ibrahim was well connected to the Royal family, and as well as placating the authorities over Sabah marrying a non-Saudi woman while being an overseas student, also got him a position in SOCO through other connections.

Sabah made a few trips to Riyadh where he met up with his younger brother Mohamed who still had fond memories of their childhood days. Then tragedy. Khalifa told Mohamed that Sabah had been murdered by an Englishman called Jason Steele. This foreigner, who also worked for SOCO, had met Sabah at several company functions and had been attracted to the English woman Sabah married. So, he took an opportunity to murder Sabah and then left Saudi with the woman called Anita. Mohamed was devastated by this news and vowed to avenge his brother's death if he ever got the chance. Khalifa was a very senior figure in the Wahhabi community and had cultivated Mohamed to become one of his trusted operators. To further his education, Khalifa arranged for him to attend the same University as Sabah and for him to concentrate in particular on nuclear Physics. Mohamed thought to himself I will have to find out more about this Doctor Steele.

Following his first day of teaching, Jason arrived home quite puzzled. Having studied his student list, he found out that Mohamed's family name was Al-Sabah. Sitting drinking a glass of wine with Anita, he asked "What was your husband Sabah's family name?" "What on earth made you think about him?" Anita replied. Jason quickly responded "It's just that in my first class today I had a Saudi student who appeared to be very religious with his facial hair and prayer beads. His name was Mohamed Al-Sabah and although he looked nothing like the Sabah I met, I sensed some connection." "Well that is a coincidence, although I do think Al-Sabah is a fairly common Saudi name. Sabah was an Al-Sabah also, but I never met a relative called Mohamed in Dhahran." Anita responded.

8

MANCHESTER, APRIL 2010

Mohamed decided to write to his uncle Khalifa to see if there was any way he could get a photograph of Jason Steele on the off chance his university lecturer and brother's murderer were the same person. Khalifa responded in a few weeks with a copy of Jason Steele's SOCO employment badge – it was the same person as his University lecturer! In addition to satisfying his uncle's request to enrol in the nuclear physics program with the goal of becoming one of Saudi's first nuclear scientists, Mohamed also had a personal vendetta to avenge his brother Sabah's murder. He reflected on his time in Manchester which had been so different to his Saudi upbringing. In Saudi, Jason Steele would have been executed for murder, but England banned the death penalty for murder in 1965.

Soon after his arrival in Manchester, Mohamed went to the Victoria Park Mosque which was very close to his rented flat. He became friendly with some of the attendees who happened to be from Pakistan and were

also studying at Manchester University. Ghulam Abbasi
became a very close friend, even though he was a Shia
Muslim and not Sunni like Mohamed. They compared
laws in England versus those in Saudi, and agreed the
stricter Sharia laws discouraged many crimes, including
stealing which often led to the guilty party having a
limb amputated in punishment. Another deterrent
was the Sharia treatment of murder, which the British
treated very leniently with no death penalty. They also
had many discussions about differences in their Islamic
beliefs, and one really intrigued Mohamed. Ghulam
invited Mohamed to join him at the Union Bar for
drinks soon after they met. After telling Ghulam he
didn't touch alcohol as it was Forbidden (Haram) in
Islam, he was surprised when Ghulam explained that
the Koran originally said that Muslims were forbidden
to attend prayers when in a drunken state. As they were
going to the bar after the Isha prayer at 7 pm., they
wouldn't be breaking any rules. Mohamed did check
his Koran, found the reference in Quran 4:43, so had
joined Ghulam and friends at the bar on Saturday
nights.

Although his experience with women was limited to
the times his uncle had taken him to the very secretive
house of ladies in Riyadh, he couldn't get over the girls
he saw in the Union Bar. Unlike the girls in Saudi,
these girls wore short skirts and revealing tops, and
commenting on this to Ghulam he was again surprised
by his new friend's comments. "Such women are classed
by us as nothing but prostitutes for dressing the way
they do. They are all available for us although we are
not allowed to marry them."

A few months later, Ghulam invited him to a special party where there would be plenty of available girls for them. The party was in a house owned by one of the senior Muslims from the community, and Mohamed was surprised to find several of his friends from the mosque along with four scantily dressed young girls sitting with the men. All were drinking alcohol, even though the girls didn't appear old enough to consume it. A few more girls came out from the kitchen and Ghulam said to Mohamed, "Take your pick and she will be only too happy to please you upstairs." Mohamed was very attracted to one of the girls who although seeming to be no more than sixteen was very well developed and had a pretty face although she had a dazed expression. Asking her name, which she said was Justine, Mohamed took her by the hand and led her upstairs to one of the empty bedrooms. Telling her to take her clothes off, he undressed and joined her on the large bed. Taking her in his arms he started kissing her when the bedroom door crashed open and two police officers came in. They told Mohamed and Justine to get dressed and led them downstairs and outside to several police vans that were already loading angry men and frightened girls. The men were being loaded on separate vans to the girls, and within minutes the house was empty.

After a thirty-minute drive, Mohamed and the five other men in his van arrived at Cheadle Heath Police Station. They were all placed into a holding cell and then one by one were booked. Mohamed was the first person taken from the holding cell and led to a police officer who told him he would be processing the group individually. "Why am I here" asked Mohamed. "Because as you already know, you are one of the grooming gang we have been chasing for the last three years. You are younger than most of the others and are not originally from Pakistan, but you were definitely involved with the underage girls at the Manchester house where you were arrested." Mohamed's pleas of innocence were ignored, and he was told to save it for the judge. The officer then took details of his name, address, contact information and listed the crime as child sexual abuse. Following his photo being taken several times and the contents of his pockets being listed and placed in a box, his fingerprints and DNA samples were taken before he was issued a prison uniform and taken to an empty holding cell. He was joined later by one of the other members of his mosque, Ahmed, who he had spoken to briefly in the past and knew he was a taxi driver. Ahmed told him to keep calm and silent, and their group's legal counsel would have them free in no time.

Unfortunately, Ahmed proved to be wrong. His court appointed defence lawyer explained to him the severity of the charges against the group, and that he was a victim of circumstances. Justine, the girl he was found with, had been kidnapped several weeks earlier. Her father happened to be a senior police officer and had a task force searching for her. She was spotted by one of her father's friends as she was entering the house where the arrests were made. The friend called the father who arranged for the house to be raided. Even though you are saying no sex took place, the father wants to make an example of you and its going to be very difficult to keep you out of prison.

"Anita, look at this!" said Jason. He handed her a copy of the Manchester Evening News which had a headline ^Grooming gang sentenced to over 100 years^. Anita read the article which described how the police had finally tracked down a grooming gang that targeted young impressionable girls, many of them under 16 years old. The gang plied them with alcohol and drugs and shared them amongst friends for sex. Twelve men were convicted of sex trafficking and other offences including rape, trafficking girls for sex and conspiracy to engage in sexual activity with a child. Of the convicted men, nine were of British Pakistani origin, two were Afghan asylum seekers, and one was a Saudi student at Manchester University. The article went on to name the culprits, included their ages of between 23 and 61, and provide details of their sentences. The ringleader, 55-year-old Khaled Amin, claimed the girls were all prostitutes, even though the youngest was only thirteen years old. He received the longest sentence of seventeen years. The remainder had lesser sentences ranging between nine and three years, with Mohamed Al Sabah being the one to receive three years for conspiracy to engage in sexual activity with a fifteen-year-old child. Although Justine had been drugged, she vaguely remembered being in bed naked with Mohamed but wasn't sure if there had been any sex. Coupled with the fact he had no previous convictions; the judge gave Mohamed the most lenient sentence and ruled that after completing his sentence he would be allowed to continue his studies at Manchester University. Anita told Jason she hoped Mohamed wasn't related to the Al Sabah family she knew as they were so kind and would be heart broken if he was their son.

9

GWADAR PAKISTAN, JANUARY 2012

Khalifa Al Sabah was tired after his trip from Riyadh to Gwadar. He was accompanied by his nephew Mohamed who recently returned to Saudi following his release from a British prison after serving a three-year sentence reduced to one and a half years for good behaviour. He was accused of having sex with a fifteen-year-old girl which would never have been a crime under Saudi Law, and which never actually happened per Mohamed. He was also accompanied by his right-hand man Mahmoud Khan who despised the West almost as much as he did. The purpose of the trip was to meet with Bin Laden's successor, Ayman Mohammed, plus other senior Al Qaeda members. Ayman was on the US list of terrorists with multimillion US dollar rewards for information leading to his capture and would not travel to many countries other than those bordering Afghanistan.

The group gathered in one of the luxurious houses in Gwadar Central, where they were drinking coffee and discussing their plans. They started with a one-minute silence in remembrance of Osama Bin Laden who orchestrated the boldest attack by Al Qaeda on America, the Great Satan, in 2001 before his murder by American troops last year. Khalifa told the group that he supplied fifteen of the martyrs involved in the attack, and the other four heroes were from the UAE, Lebanon and Egypt. He added he now had hundreds of supporters in Saudi willing to sacrifice their lives in order to rescue Saudi Arabia from the Western countries intent on stealing their oil reserves and promoting Western ideals that conflicted with Islam. When Ayman asked if he could get assistance from the Saudi Royal family, he went into a tirade about how most of the thousands of Saudi princes had been seduced by the obscene amounts of money they received. He did acknowledge there were a few of the princes who supported him, both financially and by supplying recruits to his Free Saudi Movement.

Ayman Mohammed thanked Khalifa for the support Al Qaeda received from Saudi and the Free Saudi Movement in particular. He then related his recent discussion with Osama Bin Laden prior to his murder. They had been working with their network of groups to achieve their goal of removing all foreign influences in Muslim countries. As their 2001 attack had done very little to achieve these goals, they wanted to make a dramatic attack on the Christian-Jewish alliance trying to destroy Islam that would ensure the success of their objectives. Bin Laden had been working with Muslims in the Soviet military and saw an opportunity with the dissolution of the Soviet Union in 1991. There were in excess of three thousand strategic nuclear warheads in Kazakhstan, Belarus and Ukraine. When the order came to deactivate the warheads and return them to Russia, Bin Laden worked with a small group of his followers in Ukraine to falsify documentation and steal six of the nuclear warheads. However, his followers couldn't agree on giving the weapons to Bin Laden and had been arguing for several years over how much money they could get for selling them. Bin Laden had been increasing his offer for the weapons but hadn't been able to amass the five hundred million dollars the group wanted for each warhead. Unable to use them for his 2001 attack, he came up with the plan of using four aircraft crashing into select targets for his statement to the West.

Although Bin Laden thought the 2001 attack would achieve his goals, it was apparent something more spectacular was required. So, he continued discussions with his Ukraine contacts in addition to increasing his war chest, with the hope he would be able to come to an agreement on a price for the six warheads. Ayman then explained that following Bin Laden's murder, he was contacted by a former General in the Ukraine army, Petro Kravchenko, who wanted to know if Al Qaeda had managed to raise the reduced price of two billion US dollars for the six warheads. He also explained the weapons were now in his hands and the original owners of the weapons were either dead or in prison. Ayman told the group their current war chest was around five hundred million US dollars which left a massive shortfall from the requested amount.

Khalifa told Ayman we should be checking with our other Muslim brothers for this important purchase. Hezbollah receive over one billion dollars income a year, the Taliban almost one billion a year, Hamas over half a billion and ISIS still receive over two hundred million a year. The group agreed that Ayman as the Al Qaeda leader, should approach leaders of at least the four groups mentioned as soon as an attack plan was formulated. Although the group had some disagreements, they finally agreed on a plan to detonate two warheads in the British cities of London and Manchester, and four warheads in the USA cities of New York, Los Angeles, Chicago and Houston. The attacks will take a lot of planning, but the group decided on two possible dates, March 10, 2027 to celebrate Osama Bin Laden's seventieth birthday or September 11, 2031 as the thirtieth anniversary of Osama's 2001 attack on America.

10

LONDON, JULY 2014

After four years teaching at Manchester University, Jason wanted to return to working on his long unfinished battery project. He was within a few weeks of finishing its design when he was arrested twelve years ago, and his time in Manchester had been well spent in researching recent advances in battery design. He was excited at the idea of producing a battery that would greatly reduce the need for petroleum products. Most of the developed countries were racing to cut down on carbon emissions and the development of electric cars was gaining in importance. Some countries were banning the production of petrol-powered vehicles in the very near future and increasing the power whilst miniaturizing car batteries was key to the development of an inexpensive practical electrical vehicle. He would need to recruit some key players for the project, and although Manchester University had a great Physics department, the one at Oxford University offered a larger choice of competent graduates.

Although sad to be leaving the Manchester area and its proximity to her parents, Anita didn't want to stand in the way of a project Jason was so interested in. She had never lived in the London area, and started on a project of looking for properties that would provide both comfortable accommodation as well as a place for Jason to start working on his battery project. They also needed a "granny flat" for Jason's father who agreed to join them in London as the figure head for Venus Corporation, the new company's name.

Anita provided Jason with details of three properties that met his requirements. She laid them out in order of her preferences and Jason was immediately taken by her first choice. It was a large six bedroomed country house in Henley-on-Thames with a barn conversion the previous owner used for an office as well as a storage area for boats and cars. There was also a two-bedroom guest cottage that would be ideal for David if he wanted to be separate from the main house. The property, Henley Manor, was set in four acres and the asking price was STG£ four million. Jason congratulated Anita on her find, and immediately made an offer on the property.

The next several months were spent in furnishing the properties, installing a laboratory in the barn, and settling David into his new home. He took an instant liking to the cottage and agreed that he would furnish the property and lease the home in Orinda on a fully furnished basis.

11

LONDON, JUNE 2015

Jason was admiring Da Vinci's Virgin of the Rocks in the National Gallery when a very clear "Hello Jason" came into his mind. He turned and saw an immaculately dressed man of indeterminate age standing next to him. At least two inches taller than Jason, the man reminded him of paintings he had seen depicting the Greek God Apollo. He was bronzed, muscular, and had long golden hair falling to his shoulders. "I hope I didn't startle you Jason, but I really need to take up some of your time on a very serious problem. My name is Azriel and I think you will find what I have to tell you will explain a lot of what you have been experiencing since 2009." Jason was amazed that Azriel had been able to contact him mentally, and readily agreed to talk to Azriel.

"Let's go to the coffee shop as what I have to tell you will take some time," said Azriel. Sitting at a table in the almost empty coffee shop, Azriel proceeded to tell Jason the most incredible story he had ever heard.

When he started off by telling Jason he was from the planet Elysium, 5,000 light years from Earth, Jason's initial reaction was to stand up and leave this obviously delusional person. "Please stay and listen Jason, I'm not delusional and give me thirty minutes and you will understand" came into Jason's head." "You can read my mind!" said a startled Jason. "Yes, I can, and you have the capability of doing the same," said Azriel.

Azriel then went on to tell Jason how he came from a planet thousands of years older than Earth. The planet was bigger than Earth and had a gravitational pull probably 50% stronger. Although its inhabitants looked pretty much the same, the higher gravity resulted in greater muscle development. In addition, fierce storms on Elysium led to Elysians forming much thicker skin to protect them from wind blown particles that used to cause much harm to inhabitants. Their bodies also generated protective cells centuries earlier to overcome the numerous electric storms on Elysium. These electrolyte cells were like those found in your electric eels, although much larger and able to absorb electricity. We also have telepathic capabilities and our life spans are typically one thousand earth years.

"You are probably wondering what all this has to do with me" said Azriel. "I was interested in an article written by Doctor Macintosh in the British medical journal the Lancet. I visited the doctor and he was very kind enough to provide me with a sample of your DNA. On analysis, I found a large quantity of Elysian nucleotides in your DNA, indicating one of your ancestors came from Elysium." He then continued explaining to Jason about the Traveller program of which he was a member. Some Travellers marry Terrans and in rare occasions have children. The major problem faced by Travellers is their much greater life span. They use disguises to appear to be ageing, and at the appropriate time move on to a different location and identity.

Azriel then went on to give Jason a brief history of Elysium. Thousands of years earlier, the world had been like the current day Earth. However, science and the failure of religions had a massive impact on society. The first breakthrough was in nuclear fusion technology and the ability to create nuclear fusion reactors. These reactors provided enough energy to provide Elysium's energy needs for millions of years as well as being used in interstellar space where solar energy isn't available. Eliminating all other sources of energy resulted in redirecting workforces to exploit technology in more efficient ways. For centuries we were limited in space exploration by our inability to travel at more than ten times the speed of light. We finally developed the capability to move instantaneously between any two points, regardless of distance. Although I don't understand the technology behind harnessing curved space, my hand-held portable transporter allows me to move from the Earth to Elysium in seconds. We do try to limit the usage of the transporters to one trip a month as our scientists warn us extensive use of the transporter could cause us cell problems. However, if we are forced into more frequent usage, we can check into one of our medical facilities and repair any damages fairly quickly.

Another breakthrough was in the artificial food area, and we are now able to create any food source through our replicators. They can serve us any meal or drink by voice command and have eliminated the need for the food sources you use on Earth. So, our world has no hunger, or heating and cooling needs. Currencies were eliminated centuries earlier and our government is very similar to the Earth's attempts at communism except there is just one small ruling body called the Divine Council. It's eleven members only change for health or personal reasons, and new members are voted in by the Divine Council. Crime is non-existent due to our telepathic capabilities making it impossible for people to tell lies. All citizens receive the same amount of monthly credits they can use for personal purchases which include vacations, sports events and entertainment. Accommodation is free and based on family size. In summary Elysians spend their lives as they feel fit, and many are involved in the Traveller programs among countless worlds. We still have people involved in all types of entertainment including sports, and our education system is second to none.

Azriel then explained why Jason was important to them. Following recent trends in an increased Islamic fundamentalism along with the breakup of the Soviet Union, it was becoming more likely that money hungry ex-military personnel would sell nuclear weapons to radical terrorists. This could lead to a nuclear holocaust that would turn the Earth into a dead planet, and Elysians Divine Council wanted to prevent that at all costs.

"Jason, you have presented us with an opportunity we never believed would happen. Your exposure to the electric chair resulted in your Elysium genes being reactivated. Over time you will continue to develop Elysian characteristics. However, we have medical equipment in Elysium that can immediately complete the transformation for you if you agree to accompany me there." "Azriel, I enjoy my life here and don't want to change how long I live. I'd see all my friends and family grow old and die, so thanks for the offer but I'll stay the way I am." answered Jason. Azriel was expecting a response of this nature, and before approaching Jason he received permission from the Divine Council to perform the same transformation on his wife, Anita. Nothing like this had been done before on Elysium, but to combat accidents, diseases, neurodegenerative disorders and any other medical problems, scientists developed regenerative machines that restored damaged bodies to perfect health and would be used on the couple. "Jason, I don't think you fully understand what's been happening to you. To put it simply, that electrical current kick-started the development of the Elysium genes already in your body. You are already going to outlive every human on the planet. All I am offering you is the opportunity to complete that transformation and teach you how to use your new abilities. This action would be the first time Elysium has been directly involved in another world's evolution. Because you were already transforming, I managed to convince the Divine Council to perform the same procedure on Anita. She will have to agree, but at least the two of you would be together for centuries. We will teach you how to change your appearances in order to fit in with the rest of society. The transformation will also repair any existing damage to your bodies, and you will both live long and healthy lives."

Jason returned home and had lengthy discussions with Anita on Azriel's proposal. Although she hated the thought of losing all her friends and relatives to old age, Anita decided that she would go ahead with the transformation as she did not want to lose Jason. Jason called Azriel at his hotel and agreed to go ahead, especially after Azriel told him that any children the couple had in the future would have all the characteristics of other Elysian children.

12

ELYSIUM, JUNE 2015

Azriel met Jason and Anita at his London hotel. The couple had already explained their trip to David by saying they were taking a short break on the continent, and both had packed small suitcases. Azriel told the couple that as the transporter devices operated on thought waves, they would have to hold hands this time. Once they had the normal Elysian capabilities, they would be able to transport themselves. He also warned Anita that although Jason had developed some Elysian characteristics, she would arrive in a place with a much greater gravitational pull to Earth and would find it very difficult to walk until her transformation.

In seconds the three arrived at Elysium. They materialised in the reception area of what appeared to be a reception area for a hotel or hospital. Feeling the gravitational pull, Anita quickly sat on one of the chairs in the room. Asking them to stay there for a while, Azriel excused himself and went to talk to a uniformed man standing behind a large desk which had a sign above the counter saying guest services. The receptionist pressed a button on a control panel, and a door in the wall silently opened. Two machines that resembled sophisticated MRI scanners glided through the doorway, and Azriel asked Jason and Anita to leave their suitcases where they were and lie down on the tables that appeared when the tops of the machines opened. "There is no need to remove your clothes for this procedure" said Azriel, "The enhancement machines will restructure your cells and the process will take no more than five minutes." Once they were lying down on the tables, the tops closed, Jason and Anita heard a high-pitched buzzing noise, and then they lost consciousness. Waking up the pair felt fantastic, and both heard Azriel telepathically telling them to get out of the machines.

Anita immediately noticed her feeling of heaviness had vanished and she felt better than any time she could remember. Azriel asked them to follow him and led them to an elevator that whisked them up countless floors at an incredible speed. They arrived at the thirty second floor and Azriel opened a door marked 3201, which turned out to be a large apartment very close to the elevator. Their suitcases were in the master bedroom, which was tastefully furnished with a king size bed, walk in closets, and an en-suite bathroom. One wall had the largest screen Jason had ever seen, and Azriel showed him how to operate the multi-purpose system which comprised of television, movie and news channels in addition to video capabilities with other households, hospital management, and public service facilities. Azriel showed Jason how to contact him at home, and explained the system was identical to one in the living room. The window had a panoramic view over the city, and in the living room the view was repeated. Going to the kitchen, Azriel showed Jason the food processor, explained how they simply asked for whatever they wanted, and the meal or drink would appear in seconds. He also showed them the recycling processor and after ensuring they were both happy to be left alone, said he would meet up with them later for dinner.

The next few days were filled with instructions by Azriel on what to expect from their mutated bodies. The biggest change was their telepathic capability. In addition to having total recall and being able to play over everything they ever experienced in their minds, they were also able to pass that experience on to others. They learned to read each other's minds, but also block out the countless thoughts coming to them from others unless they specifically wanted to hear them. They also learned to direct their thoughts to the transporter devices and were amazed at how easy it was to move from point A to point B. Azriel explained how he had their scientists adapt a working iPhone to incorporate the transporter and all they had to do when they returned home was put their own chip into the new phones.

Azriel then went on to a brief description of how all their senses had been enhanced:

Hearing for humans was in the range of 20 hertz to 20 kilohertz, whereas their range had been increased to 300 kilohertz.

Sight was about eight times greater than humans with the added telescopic capability of being able to zoom in on objects.

Sense of smell was at least five times as strong as humans.

The sense of taste was well over ten times that of humans.

The sense of touch was not only greater than in humans but there was the added ability of being able to feel things at a distance without even touching them.

Their blood types were now the same as all other Elysians, meaning they can all give and receive blood from each other. In addition, compared to Terran blood, the oxygen-carrying capacity of haemoglobin was greatly increased to provide their increased musculature with the needed additional oxygen.

The enhanced physical capabilities due to their increased muscle size included a top running speed of fifty miles per hour, over twice as fast as any human. Their skin was now capable of stopping a bullet, something Jason had considered while watching a spider spinning a web in his prison cell. Finishing his explanation of physical differences they now had, Azriel showed them how to disguise their age with both makeup and clothing so people wouldn't notice their increased lifespans.

Although Jason was amazed at the physical improvements, he still had many questions. One thing that did not make sense was when Azriel was telling them about previous travellers. "Azriel, I think that I will be putting myself into some physical danger if I will be involved with extremely dangerous terrorists.

You mentioned that Jesus Christ was one of the many Travellers sent to Earth, but history books have him being killed in a barbaric way. How was that possible if he had more strength and extra strong skin?" "Jesus used his telepathic capabilities to make all the people involved in his "death" to believe what they were trying to do. In reality he wasn't injured but with so many people being against him, the Council at the time decided it would be better for him to appear to have been killed then bring him back to Elysium." explained Azriel. A few other things regarding your protection. I will be giving both of you key rings that contain a small flashlight. Although the light works, you can use your telepathic capabilities to turn the beam into a ray that will freeze the nervous system for any living creature that has a nervous system. When you switch the effect off, the creature(s) will not remember anything about their being frozen.

Once their initiation was complete, Azriel took them on a tour of the city which also raised numerous questions.

Why were there roads and electric cars when people could travel anywhere using their transporters? In addition, how are the cars able to travel through the air? Many people still enjoyed the old-fashioned transportation methods for recreation, even though cars were driverless explained Azriel. The anti-gravity features in cars made them capable of flight as well as driving on roadways. They are also capable of travelling underwater.

Why were there still shopping malls when you have machines to make anything? Again, for recreational purposes only.

Do people still work? After finishing the mandatory schooling, people could choose an occupation either in the science field, historical research, health services, construction, entertainment or the Traveller program. There were also many people involved in service industries in support of schools, shops, hotels and other leisure activities. Many people worked in the entertainment industry, including sports people, film and television, music and art. Working people receive additional credits to the standard credits given to all people. We have eliminated salaries, money, banking etc and every person receives sufficient credits to live a comfortable life without working if they choose to do so.

Would it be possible for me to spend some time with your scientists to find out what I can about battery miniaturization? I'm afraid that would be a step the Divine Council would definitely refuse. However, with your background and increased brain capacity, I have no doubt you will solve that problem in the very near future.

Still having endless questions, Jason and Anita were told they now had to return to Earth as there were imminent dangers that only they could resolve. Thinking themselves back to their home, they surprised David by materialising in the living room!

13

LONDON, JUNE 2015

"Where on Earth did you come from?" asked David. "I never heard you come in." "I guess we are moving quieter than ever dad" said Jason. Azriel's last instruction had been never to reveal anything about him or Elysium to anyone, including close family members. "How was your very short trip?" asked David. "Even that short break really rejuvenated us. We will definitely go for a longer time when we can afford the time for a break," said Jason.

Working in his laboratory, Jason was filled with regret about not being given access to the technical capabilities on Elysium. They had perfected and greatly enhanced everything Jason was working on and being able to talk to one of their scientists would have saved him years of research into the ideal miniature battery. His time spent at Manchester University exposed him to the potential use of nanotechnology in battery production, and this potential for an even smaller and more powerful battery was all he could think about. Knowing that scientists in another planet had solved all the problems he faced made him determined to succeed.

"He must be working in that barn" flashed through Jason's mind. Wondering where the thought came from, he focused on the person and could immediately read his mind. It was Mohamed al Sabah and he had found Jason and was going to kill him. Jason stood behind the barn door, and when Mohamed slowly opened the door, grabbed the gun out of his hand and sat him down in a chair. "What are you doing here?" asked Jason. When Mohamed told him he was here to avenge the murder of his older brother Sabah, Jason remembered what Azriel taught him. Thinking back to the scene at the Al-Oasis compound when Sabah was murdered by Khalifa, Jason replayed the scene in Mohamed's mind. "That can't be true" yelled Mohamed, "How can you put such lies in my head?" Jason then replayed the scene where Khalifa murdered Makram and started explaining things to Mohamed.

"Your uncle Khalifa is the head of the Free Saudi Movement dedicated to removing all foreigners from Saudi Arabia. He is very religious, although true Muslims believe Islam is a religion of peace that teaches against killing, especially of innocent people. He was infuriated when your brother Sabah married a Christian girl against the family's wishes and considered his actions against Sabah an honour killing. He thought he had killed the wife as well, but she luckily survived." Jason could feel Mohamed's thoughts changing as he took in the scenes in his mind as well as Jason's words.

In addition to being highly intelligent, Jason sensed Mohamed was a caring person and truly regretted his purpose for coming to Jason's home.

"Let's go into the house and you can meet Sabah's ex-wife and she can tell you more about her time with Sabah" said Jason. So, the pair entered the house and Anita greeted Mohamed like a long-lost brother. Mohamed was overwhelmed by this attractive caring couple and immediately liked David when Jason introduced him to his father. David explained to Mohamed how he thought he had lost his son when he was framed for his wife and daughter's murder, and that it was a miracle he survived death by electrocution. Anita told Mohamed how she met Sabah and how happy she had been with him. She also liked Sabah's parents but hadn't met Mohamed's mother. She was devastated when Khalifa murdered Sabah and vowed to avenge his death, although meeting and falling in love with Jason had lessened her thoughts of revenge.

Jason then went on to explain why he had been framed for the murders, and said although he could understand the Saudi fear that his miniature battery would cause havoc to their oil industry, it was simply a matter of time before things changed. In 2003 when his family was murdered, electric cars were things of the future. Twelve years later many countries are talking about stopping production of petrol cars to combat global warming. Even the battery he was about to produce was now outdated with advances in nanotechnology.

"I've started a company here with the intent of producing a new type of battery far smaller and more powerful than those in existence today. I remember you as a student of mine in Manchester and would really like you to consider joining my company on this adventure". Mohamed was shocked by this offer. He explained how he was working with his uncle's group on an important project and doubted if they would let him leave them. Reading Mohamed's mind, Jason was horrified to learn the important project involved setting off nuclear explosions in two countries, but that Mohamed was now indecisive after finding out his uncle had killed Sabah. Although he was familiar with honour killings which happened all the time in Saudi, being lied to by his uncle in addition to him murdering his favourite brother was causing him to have second thoughts.

"I'd like to hear about your uncle's project and see if there is any way I can be of assistance" said Jason. When Mohamed remained silent, Jason said "Let me guess. I know your uncle thought highly of Osama Bin Laden and his belief that his actions in 2001 would lead to a mass exodus of foreigners from Saudi, that never happened. I imagine your uncle is plotting something similar. I do know you were enrolled in the Nuclear program at the university, and that is one way to reduce the demand for fossil fuels. The West is pushing for renewable energy, and it won't be very long before the demand for oil will be a thing of the past. So, your uncle's efforts are really wasted as the foreigners in Saudi are there primarily for the oil industry. Another thing your uncle needs to take into consideration is the spread of Islam in the West. Saudi has been generous in providing money for mosques, and there are now over 1,500 in the UK and over 2,000 in the USA. There are over two and a half million Muslims in the UK and three and a half million in the USA. In Manchester where we used to live, there are close to four hundred thousand Muslims and there are well over one million living in London. There are even more living in major cities in the USA. So, attacking the population in those countries could result in the murder of countless innocent Muslims which goes completely against Islam. I do know the Muslim population in the UK was around 200,000 when I was born in 1970 and it's now over three million. It is projected to be the largest religion in the UK with around thirteen million in 2050. So whatever your uncle is plotting, I suggest you leave his group and join me."

Mohamed realised what his uncle and friends were planning was horrific. He had many friends in the Manchester mosque and a nuclear bomb detonation in Manchester would instantly kill everyone in the city centre. The fireball would cover not only the city centre, but Manchester University and several train stations as well. Radiation would kill up to 90% of the people in Old Trafford, Stretford, Prestwich, Salford and Pendlebury. The air blast would kill almost 100% of the people in places like Stockport and Middleton, and the secondary air blast would kill most people in places like Bolton and Rochdale. Thermal radiation would give third degree burns to people in places as far away as Sheffield and the Peak District. Adding London and the four largest cities in the US to the equation, the plans would kill several million people and probably 20% of them would be peaceful Muslims. Mohamed had to stop this at any cost.

"Jason, my uncle is plotting to explode six nuclear warheads in London, Manchester and the four largest cities in the USA. His group do not have the warheads now but have been planning to obtain them for several years. They are stockpiling diamonds to purchase the warheads from a group in Ukraine who acquired them over ten years earlier when the Soviet Union broke up and are selling them to the highest bidder. Al Qaeda, who my uncle is working with, have agreed on a price of two billion US dollars for the six warheads. With the help of other Islamic groups including the Taliban, they have accumulated three quarters of the needed diamonds and expect to have all of them within one year. I am one of the six Muslims with the needed Nuclear training to oversee the placement and explosion of the warheads. I must have been crazy to agree to participate in this atrocity and will do everything in my power to stop it."

Jason was relieved by Mohamed's speech, and his ability to read Mohamed's mind confirmed his willingness to follow through on his words. Finding out that Mohamed and a few others including his uncle were living in a rented house in Bell Street, Marylebone, Jason asked what the team did while they were waiting to acquire the warheads. Mohamed explained to Jason that his studies at Manchester University had been interrupted in 2010 when he foolishly went to a friend's house and was arrested for being found in bed with an underage girl. He served 18 months of a 3-year jail sentence being released early for good behaviour. His uncle called him back to Saudi, and in 2012 took him on a trip where they met with the leader of Al Qaeda and started planning the nuclear attacks. He returned to Manchester later that year and recently finished his bachelor's degree in physics. His uncle asked him to join the small planning group in London which he did last month. Although his uncle spent most of his time fund raising in the Middle East, he was asked to stay in London with two other members of the group to be available for whatever tasks his uncle assigned. Mohamed being the senior member of the group after his uncle, had the additional job of staying in touch with a senior member of the Saudi Consulate in London. Abdul Karim, one of Khalifa's dedicated followers, had been posted to a junior position in the Consulate in 2009 and had risen to become assistant to Prince Sultan, the Minister of Foreign Affairs.

"When your uncle returns to London, I would still like you to ask his approval to join my company. You can explain it is a development company in the power industry, and you may be able to make contacts to further his goals." Mohamed said he would try, and after giving him his mobile phone number and returning his gun, Jason said goodbye to Mohamed and hoped he would hear from him in the very near future.

14

LONDON, JULY 2015

Jason and Richard retired to the library after a very enjoyable dinner with their wives and David. Richard James was their closest neighbour, in addition to being the current Chief Executive of MI6, the United Kingdom's foreign intelligence agency. With an annual budget approaching three billion pounds and some 2,500 employees, Jason thought Richard would be the best person to talk to about Mohamed's revelations. Although initially dubious about Jason's story, Richard took a keen interest on hearing details of Khalifa's meeting with Ayman Mohammed, the man who replaced Osama Bin Laden as head of Al Qaeda. "We did hear rumours about missing nuclear warheads years ago, but they were dismissed when nothing concrete came from our intelligence operators' investigations into the rumours. We believe the black-market price for a nuclear warhead would be in the five hundred million pounds region, so a two-billion-pound price for six warheads is feasible.

Do you have any details on the sellers?" Jason replied that he didn't but was so concerned about the potential attack he was going to do whatever he could to find out details. Richard warned Jason not to investigate further into the matter as it was extremely dangerous and should be left to people with the correct training and experience. Jason explained to Richard that he had a personal relationship with Mohamed and was hoping he would join his company. He did not think assigning an MI6 operator to question Mohamed would be wise, as his uncle Khalifa would have no hesitation in executing Mohamed if he thought he would jeopardize Al Qaeda's plans. Richard agreed that if Mohamed did join the Venus Corporation, he would use Jason to keep him informed of any new developments. However, if Mohamed didn't join the company, he would have no option but to bring him in for questioning.

A week later Mohamed called and said his uncle had agreed to him joining the Venus Corporation. During that week, Jason discovered that Azriel hadn't told him about all the new capabilities he'd acquired in Elysium. He could read books far faster than ever before, and he had always been a fast reader with the capability to retain what he'd read. He decided to read the Koran in full and was amazed to finish reading it as well as being able to recall all the text in less than an hour. He'd also noticed while working on his battery design that the latest discoveries in nanotechnology were obvious and easy to understand. He knew it wouldn't be long before he finished the battery design. Jason had been thinking that his next move would be to find out all he could about the planned nuclear attacks and prevent them. An idea was forming in his mind, but he needed to check a few things out with Azriel to see if it would work. Thinking about Azriel, he formed a question and Azriel responded immediately. "I didn't go into detail about the transporter as there were a lot more basic things to cover in the short time you were on Elysium. Although we held hands the first time, we don't need to do that. We only need to think about where we want to go, and the portable transporter takes us there." When Jason asked if he could go anywhere, Azriel explained the travel section in Elysium libraries. "They are arranged by planet, and have pictures of all places of interest, major cities etc and once we store the picture in our memories we can then travel there whenever we want. You will also find details of the planet's climate and the best time to visit. It will also recommend the appropriate skin colour." "What do you mean by that?" asked Jason. "As our sun is much stronger than the sun on Earth, our melanocytes can produce different amounts and kinds of melanin that we can select based on the strength of a planet's sun. You can turn your skin from being very white to very black and any shade in between by your thought process." "Can we also transport items larger than the suitcases we took to Elysium?" "Yes, you can take anything transportable within your range of vision." " One other capability I forgot to mention is you now have the ability to hold your breath for as long as five hours, based on the amount of energy you are using. If you were using your maximum amount of energy, that time would drop considerably to around two hours. That is still longer than the up to two minutes the average human on Earth manages. I believe the longest recorded time for a human on Earth holding their breath is twenty-four minutes, considerably more than the average but still a long way to go compared to the average Elysian." Jason thanked Azriel and ended his telepathic conversation.

Jason went over his plan of action and realised it should be easier than he first thought. He would change his appearance, using brown contact lenses and dyeing his hair black. He could then use the newly discovered capability to turn his skin a dark brown colour and join the mosque Mohamed worships at. He would obtain documentation to show he was a Saudi and with his Arabic speaking capabilities plus knowledge of the Koran, he didn't think anyone would believe he was anyone other than who he claimed to be. He would then have Mohamed introduce him to his uncle Khalifa as his Nuclear Physics Lecturer. It would then be up to him to convince Khalifa they shared the same beliefs in freeing Saudi of Westerners and try to get included in Khalifa's team. He could then explain to Khalifa that nuclear weapons require routine maintenance and if these weapons were over twenty years old, they should be checked by a nuclear scientist to see if they would still work before buying them. If he could get Khalifa to take him to inspect the weapons, he would be able to transport them to a different location later.

15

LONDON, SEPTEMBER 2015

"Uncle, I would like to introduce you to my former physics lecturer, Doctor Suleiman Hussain, who is originally from Tabuk but studied in America." "Assalaam alaikum" said Khalifa, shaking Jason's hand. "Wa 'alaikum assalaam" responded Jason. "You are indeed very fortunate to have such a remarkable nephew. He was the top student in my classes, and I predict a very promising future for him. ""You are very kind Doctor Hussain," responded Khalifa, "The family is extremely proud of his achievements. I'm from the Riyadh area and have never been to Tabuk where I believe you even have snow in the winter." "Yes" said Jason, "although I saw a lot more snow during my stay in Manchester." Jason then went on to tell Khalifa how his parents sent him to study at the Massachusetts Institute of Technology (MIT) in Cambridge Massachusetts where he earned a doctoral degree in nuclear engineering, although he was lecturing in advanced electricity and magnetism in Manchester.

They parted on friendly terms, and saw each other the following Fridays at the mosque, from where they went to a coffee shop after the services and had lengthy discussions on Saudi Arabia, religion, and the decadent way of life in the West. Agreeing that Shariah law would greatly improve life in the West, they concluded it would be many years before that could be accomplished in the UK, and probably never in the USA. Even though there were more Muslims in America, they only represented just over 1% of the population. This compared to nearly 6% of the population in England, and a recent study showed that 43% of all migrants to the UK in the last five years were Muslim. Although the Mayor of London, Boris Johnson, said this year that he was opposed to a Shariah system running in parallel with UK justice, several years earlier the former Archbishop of Canterbury, Rowan Williams, suggested it was inevitable that elements of Sharia would be incorporated into British Law. By last year there were around 85 "sharia courts" in the UK, operated by the Islamic Sharia Council and the smaller Muslim Arbitration Council. On their fourth meeting, Khalifa asked Jason what he thought about the Western influence in Saudi Arabia. Jason responded he couldn't wait for their presence to end there at which time he would undoubtably return to his homeland.

The following week Khalifa asked Jason if he would like to join them at his apartment after services for dinner and to meet other like-minded Saudis. Jason readily agreed and was delighted when Khalifa began the conversation by talking about plans that Al Qaeda had for driving all foreigner out of Saudi Arabia.

When Khalifa mentioned the possibility of acquiring nuclear weapons, Jason said that sounded like a pipe dream as only a few countries had that capability and their weapons storage facilities were heavily guarded. Khalifa then explained they were amassing funds to buy six nuclear weapons from a group that came into possession of them in 1994. They expected to have the total cost within two years and then would decide how and if the weapons would be used. This gave Jason the opportunity to ask how the weapons were stored and what type of maintenance was being followed. When Khalifa asked why was that important, Jason replied the weapons deteriorate over age, and that Khalifa should have them checked before making any purchases.

After Jason left the group to return home, Khalifa asked Mohamed if he would be able to inspect the weapons to see if they were still operational. Mohamed said that he didn't think he would be able to perform such an inspection but had no doubt that Suleiman could. On being asked by Khalifa if Suleiman could be trusted, Mohamed said I am certain we can trust him as he feels the same way we do about the Western influence in Saudi Arabia. He further added that we don't need to tell Suleiman about our plans for the weapons as that is still a long way in the future and he won't be involved in that operation. Khalifa asked Jason if he would be willing to inspect the weapons when they met at the mosque the following week and Jason said certainly. On asking where the weapons were stored, Khalifa told him they were in a small city in the Ukraine. Even though reading people's minds did not require understanding their language, Jason decided with his new capabilities he would spend the few hours it would take him to learn the Ukrainian language. Searching through the different courses, he decided to purchase courses from two companies. He initially was attracted to the Rosetta Stone courses where he could purchase their unlimited access to 24 different languages, but unfortunately, they did not include Ukrainian. So, in addition to Rosetta Stone he signed up for the Ukrainian language course in Duolingo. Although the basic language course was free, it contained ads which would slow things down, so he signed up for the Duolingo Plus which had a small monthly fee but was ad free along with other benefits.

16

DNIPRO UKRAINE, NOVEMBER 2015

Jason, Khalifa and Mohamed arrived in Dnipro Ukraine after a gruelling sixteen-hour flight from London via Vienna. They took a taxi to their hotel, the Reikartz Dnipro, where they had two rooms reserved. Khalifa went to the room he was sharing with Mohamed and told Jason to meet them in the lobby in 30 minutes when they would go out for dinner. Their host, Petro Kravchenko, was picking them up at 9am the following morning to take them to see the weapons. He apologised for being busy in the evening so wouldn't be able to join them for dinner. However, he recommended their eating at the Arizona Food Bar which was only a short walk from the hotel.

The restaurant was classed as American, Mexican and Steakhouse, and had a well-stocked bar even including draft Guinness. Mohamed had warned Jason about his uncle's dislike of alcohol and how he considered it haram for all Muslims. The tables were spaced out, so it was easy to have a quiet conversation. Although the menu seemed to be basically burgers and steaks, Jason was very happy with his steak order which was cooked medium rare, exactly as requested. Jason was surprised to see his companions ordering burritos but was impressed when they arrived. They ordered San Francisco style burritos which were stuffed to the brim with various fillings including beef, rice, beans, sour cream, cheese and more. Service was quick, and they were impressed with the attentive staff, many of whom spoke English.

The next morning Petro was waiting for them in the hotel reception area. He was a very athletic looking man who seemed to be out of place in civilian clothing. Wasting no time, he led them out to a large SUV with tinted glass windows. There were already three men in the SUV which was an eight-seater, and while Jason and his friends took the back-bench seat, Petro apologised and said the three visitors would have to be blindfolded. Although the storage place for the weapons was guarded 24 hours a day and had a complete security system including cameras and motion sensors, they were taking no chances with such valuable items. The journey to the storage site took over thirty minutes, and Jason was glad of his Ukrainian lesson as he was able to understand the guards small talk which consisted mainly about their favourite soccer team which seemed to be Dynamo Kyiv. They were also talking about rumours of a team from Dnipro being formed but thought that would be a few years away.

Once they arrived at the site, they were led into the storage facility and then had their blindfolds removed. Jason had a holdall containing his equipment which included a Geiger counter, and said to the group it may be better if I inspect the weapons on my own. Khalifa and Mohamed agreed, but Petro said he would accompany Jason and his men would stay with the other two.

Jason was impressed by the fire safety designs in the building, and after checking the six warheads announced his satisfaction that they were in working order. The process took just over an hour, and they were back at their hotel by noon, having been blindfolded for their return trip. Thanking Petro for his assistance, Khalifa said he was impressed by the security measures in place. He also questioned the ages of Petro and his associates, as they couldn't possibly have been involved in the weapons acquisition over twenty years earlier. Petro smiled and said my father was a Colonel in the Ukrainian ground forces and along with six of his closest friends moved the weapons at the fall of the Soviet Union. Their group now consisted of more than thirty soldiers and ex-soldiers who were involved in the operation. They spent many years deliberating over how they could sell the weapons and had agreed to sell them to Osama Bin Laden once he had accumulated their asking price. As Bin Laden was killed before he could finalise the deal, they were now working with Ayman and were confident of his ability to raise the money in the very near future.

Once Petro departed, Khalifa called the airlines and changed their flights to the afternoon having finished their business far sooner than anticipated. He also called Ayman Mohammed and told him their nuclear physics expert, Doctor Suleiman Hussain, had inspected the weapons and was satisfied they were still operational. Ayman thanked Khalifa and told him that thanks to the Islamic State in Iraq, he expected to achieve the weapons purchase price within six months, having one and a half billion dollars' worth of diamonds already. As this is far sooner than originally expected, they may want to bring their planned attack dates forward. Khalifa agreed and said let me check with my contacts and see what I can come up with.

17

LONDON, NOVEMBER 2015

Jason still in his Arab disguise went to see Richard James soon after his return from Ukraine. He explained to Richard that he had been accepted by the terrorist group as a nuclear weapons expert and the Ukrainians had taken the group to view the weapons which were in a storage facility in Ukraine. They were viable nuclear warheads and the facility was very well guarded. He told how they were all blindfolded when taken to the weapons, but he thought he would be able to locate the facility if he had to. "Well you certainly look the part" said Richard. "If I hadn't recognized your voice I would never have believed it was you." "I am trying to work out if there is any way to relieve the group of the weapons but if I could retrieve them from the storage facility, the question is what would I do with them?" Richard thought for a while and said "The weapons should have been turned in to the Russian military with all the other nuclear weapons from the former Soviet States. How that could be accomplished

I really don't know. I do have a contact in the Russian Embassy who is their senior FSB (Russian Federal Security Service, formerly the KGB) agent although his title in the Embassy is Senior Counsellor – Political affairs. We have worked well together on a number of sensitive operations and I know he would keep this situation completely to himself."

Jason agreed with Richard who arranged for them to meet with his contact, Alexei Federov, at Richard's favourite club, White's in St. James. As the oldest gentlemen's club in London, White's still maintains its tradition as a club for men only. Jason was surprised a men's only club still existed in London, and Richard told him how the clubs former chairman resigned after 15 years in the position because the club declined to admit women. Richard booked one of their several private rooms where the three of them could have an uninterrupted meal. Deciding he would be better off going to the meeting as Jason Steele, he quickly changed his appearance and Suleiman Hussein was temporarily put on hold.

Alexei turned out to be an impeccably dressed man in his early 50's. He still had a full head of greying hair, looked very fit, and spoke English without a trace of an accent. When Jason asked about his youthful appearance, Alexei told him that in addition to his daily swimming and weight training regimes, he still trained weekly in both judo and karate, and was a 9th dan black belt in both disciplines. The conversation slowly turned around to the breakup of the Soviet Union, and Richard asked Alexei if he ever heard rumours about missing soviet nuclear weapons. Jason noticed Alexei seemed a little hesitant when he answered I don't believe so. Jason then recounted that when he was working in Saudi Arabia, he became fluent in Arabic, and overheard a couple of senior Saudis talking about the possible purchase of six nuclear warheads from Ukraine. Alexei admitted hearing some rumours but discounted them immediately. He explained how strict the return of weapons from former States had been, and there would have to be several senior military personnel involved in falsifying documentation to achieve such a theft. Not only were senior Russians involved, but the United States sponsored the National Defense Authorization Act which provided US funding for the removal of nuclear weapons to carefully guarded sites. They were heavily involved in efforts to prevent the sale or illegal dispersal of the weapons, and certified that all such weapons had been safely transferred to Russia.

Jason asked if he could visit the storage sites as being a professor of nuclear physics, he was curious to see a nuclear storage facility. Alexei explained that was impossible due to the strict security involved, but he did have a recent video taken of the facility which he was welcome to view. Jason thanked Alexei and they arranged to meet up at the Russian Embassy the following day.

The Russian Embassy in London is in Kensington Palace Gardens and Alexei met Jason and Richard at the entrance to the building and escorted them through the security check, and after a short walk to Alexei's impressive office. In addition to a large antique wooden desk with a comfortable leather office chair and two visitor chairs, there was a sitting section with more leather seating, a hand carved coffee table and a large screen television set. After setting his guests up with coffees, Alexei turned the TV on and ran the short video for them. The facility had ground floor administrative offices, but the actual storage area was underground and had many storage bays housing the nuclear weapons. Alexei explained that the structures were reinforced concrete containment structures designed to withstand both interior and exterior explosions. The facility had numerous emergency systems including a lightning protection system, fire protection systems, and a 1,000 KW emergency generator. The building was surrounded by a perimeter fence, had four security guard towers, patrol roads which were constantly checked and with the large number of armed security personnel both inside and outside the storage facility appeared well protected.

Having seen the video and following a lengthy talk for Alexei on how seriously the Russian government took the safeguarding of nuclear facilities, Jason and Richard thanked him for his time and said they were impressed with the security measures they had witnessed.

Returning home, Jason decided to move the six weapons from Ukraine to one of the empty storage bays he noticed in the Russian facility. It was amazingly simple to think of the Ukraine facility, materialise there, include the weapons in his transportation to the Russian site, then transport himself back to his home. The whole process took less than ten minutes and Jason was finding it hard to believe the fantastic capabilities he'd received from Elysium.

Jason called on Richard to update him on the weapons status. "I can't explain how they have done it, but I have some confidential contacts who managed to remove the nuclear weapons from Ukraine and deposit them in a Russian nuclear arms storage site containing the rest of the weapons recovered from the Ukraine. Although they required complete confidentiality, I am concerned that my involvement may become known to the Ukrainian military personnel who were selling the weapons as well as the terrorist group who wanted to buy them. I want to protect Mohamed from any fallout from the exercise, but I may need your help in arresting the rest of the terrorist gang once I have some firm evidence." "Jason, it sounds as if you are getting too involved with these people. They are extremely dangerous and should be left to the professionals to deal with." was Richard's response. Jason explained that he was already too deeply involved to just walk away from the situation.

The following day Richard came to see Jason in his home. "Jason, I've been giving a lot of thought to your predicament and I've concluded that it may be beneficial for me to offer you a position in MI6. I should first explain that we have always been called the Secret Intelligence Service (SIS) although the term MI6 came into use at the start of World War 2. Our people work secretly around the world to make the UK a safer place and one of our three core aims is to stop terrorism. Your experience and language skills make you a perfect candidate for our organization, and I would like to assure you that contrary to popular belief, although our work is secret, everything we do is legal.

Although I'm sure you don't need it, we would offer you the salary and position of special intelligence officer reporting directly to me. You don't have to give me an answer now, but I would like you to seriously consider the offer." "Richard, I am more than pleased to accept the position. There is nothing more important to me than the safety of our country." said Jason.

A few weeks later Richard had a phone call from Alexei telling him about a strange event at the same nuclear storage facility he recently showed Richard and Jason on video tape. One of their storage bays believed to be empty recently reported an additional six nuclear weapons. They were part of the large transfer of weapons from Ukraine years earlier but had been missing from the transfer papers in a presumed human recording error. Although there was extensive security at the storage site, its purpose was to prevent the theft of weapons. Additional security measures had been implemented to check all items coming into the site.

18

DNIPRO UKRAINE,
DECEMBER 2015

Petro was furious with his security guards. Although they had four guards on eight hour shifts every day, they only inspected the weapons inside the facility on a weekly basis. The senior officer for the weekly inspection called Petro at home and told him they had a massive problem and he needed to come to the site immediately. On arriving, Petro was faced with the impossible situation of the nuclear weapons storage bay being empty. Facing the twelve guards plus four senior officers, he kept asking why no one had noticed the weapons being removed from the facility. Although the guards were fearful of Petro's reaction, they all agreed no one had seen any movement and all insisted they had been fully alert during their watch. When Petro asked the guards to run the security tapes for the previous week, they found one two-minute section they couldn't believe. Petro called the manager of the security company responsible for all their cameras and ordered him to report to the facility immediately. When he arrived, they showed him the two-minute section and asked for an explanation. The tape showed Suleiman Hussein's sudden appearance in the storage area, him walking over to the nuclear weapons, and then him suddenly vanishing along with the weapons. Scratching his head in disbelief, the security manager could only tell Petro that there was no fault with his security cameras and video footage, but he had no idea how they were witnessing what the tape showed. "I could understand it if it was a movie with all the trick photography they can use, but I've no idea about what I've just seen." Petro thanked him for coming so quickly and said we will take it from here.

With nothing to go on apart from the short sight of Suleiman Hussein, Petro called for five of his top men and explained the situation. "We have a two-billion-dollar investment that has just vanished, and we must get it back. The only clue we have is this guy Suleiman Hussein appearing on the video. He came over with Khalifa and his nephew who are based in London. You will join me in travelling to London and finding out how they have managed to pull this robbery off." Splitting the men into two separate groups, he booked three people on two different flights to London the following day. Reluctantly, Petro decided to make a call to Ayman to report the missing weapons. "The weapons have been stolen and we don't know how it happened apart from the fact that the man Khalifa brought to inspect the weapons appears to be involved. I need your help in trying to get to the bottom of this. First, I need Khalifa's address in London and want you to tell him to be available for a meeting with us on Friday at 6pm. I know they go to the mosque for prayers at that time, but it is important for him to stay and be available for us with his nephew Mohamed as well. He must also make sure his flat mates go to the mosque as they normally do. Secondly I need you to arrange for firearms for the six of us travelling to London." "I am devastated to hear about this and have no doubt that Khalifa would never be involved in such actions. I thought his nephew was also dedicated to our cause as well." said Ayman. "Be assured I will make the calls. The largest armoury in London is at the main mosque and I will tell the Imam to expect you there on Thursday evening." Petro was satisfied with the arrangements and hoped the trip tomorrow would solve the puzzle of the missing weapons.

19

LONDON, JANUARY 2016

P etro and his group landed within half an hour of each other on a cold and gloomy winter's day. They were booked in the London Central Travelodge Marylebone which was a five-minute walk from Khalifa's address. Petro asked the group to stay in their rooms while he went to meet the Imam of the London Central Mosque. Although it was only a 15-minute walk, Petro took a taxi there because of the weather. He was impressed by the size of the mosque which is located on the edge of Regent's Park in central London. Petro met the Imam, Ahmed Hussain, at the mosque entrance and was led through two sets of doors and down a flight of stairs to several offices and storage rooms below ground. Ahmed unlocked a door to the armoury and told Petro to enter and take whatever he needed. He simply asked for Petro to return the items after he had finished with them. Petro went into the well-stocked room and from a wide range of handguns selected six Glock 17's. Although originally manufactured for the Austrian military, their use was extended to law enforcement officers and military personnel around the world due to their reliability, magazine capacity of 17 rounds in a standard magazine and their low weight. His team were all familiar with the Glock 17, and he took several boxes of 9x19mm Parabellum cartridges for the empty guns. He hoped the guns wouldn't be necessary, but he was taking no chances in his attempt to recover their nuclear weapons.

Returning to the hotel, Petro gave each member of his team a fully loaded gun with two spare cartridges and briefed them on his plans for the following day. After renting an SUV large enough for the six of them, they would travel to Bell Street in the late afternoon. Four men would remain in the car while Petro and one person went into Khalifa's house. If they hadn't returned to the car in thirty minutes, the rest of the group were to force their way into the house to see what the problem was. If more time was needed, Petro would come back to the car and update them. And of course, if they heard any gunfire, they were to come into the house immediately.

Arriving at Bell Street the next day, Petro and Borys, his second in command, knocked on the door and were immediately let in by Mohamed. Walking into the cheaply furnished living room, Khalifa welcomed Petro saying it was nice to see him again and asked how he could be of assistance. "Khalifa, I have a major problem," began Petro. "Soon after your visit to inspect the nuclear weapons they vanished." "But how could that happen with your very efficient security?" asked Khalifa. "We have no explanation for the theft.

However, our security cameras picked up a very brief image of your Doctor Suleiman Hussein more than a week after your visit. The camera showed him in the room with the weapons and next he and the weapons were gone." But that seems impossible," said Khalifa, "Doctor Hussein is a respected lecturer and Mohamed was in one of his classes. We met frequently at the mosque as well as socially. He shared all the values we do, and I can't believe he would do anything to jeopardize our purchase of the weapons."

"Mohamed, is there anything further you know about Doctor Hussein? I don't even know where he lives." asked Khalifa. "No uncle you know as much as I do" stammered a visibly shaken Mohamed. "Mohamed, you have lived with me for most of your life and I know when you aren't telling me everything" said Khalifa. "That is all I know uncle, I swear it" said Mohamed. "Mohamed, I think your uncle is right and you aren't telling us the truth. I'll give you ten seconds to change your mind" said Petro. "There really is nothing more to tell" said Mohamed. "Well Mohamed you are one very lucky person. In the old days we would have used a lot of physical persuasion methods to get the truth from you. That would have been very painful for you as well as time consuming. However, I'm going to give you an injection of sodium thiopental which will have you cooperating with us in less than a minute. Roll his sleeve up Khalifa." said Petro.

Petro told Khalifa he would give Mohamed an initial dose of 210 mg but would add more if they didn't get the desired results. In less than a minute after the dose was administered, Mohamed started giggling and appeared to be intoxicated. He developed a warm and friendly feeling towards Petro and asked him how he could help him. Petro said "I'd like to learn a bit more about your friend Doctor Hussein." Mohamed laughed and said, "He is probably the smartest person I ever met and was a fantastic lecturer." Petro said that was strange as they had no record of a Doctor Hussein at Manchester University when you were there." Oh no silly," laughed Mohamed, "his real name is Jason Steele and he only used the Doctor Hussein name to meet friends at the mosque we all attend." When asked what Jason Steele did, Mohamed said "He is my employer as the boss of Venus Corporation where we are developing a miniature battery that will be the smallest most powerful battery in the world."

Petro thanked Mohamed and left the room with Khalifa. "He won't remember any of this conversation when he regains his senses" said Petro. "I'd like you to keep quiet about it all as we may need to ask more questions later. Asking Khalifa to make sure he and Mohamed stayed in the house for the next few days, Petro and Borys returned to the car. After a few telephone calls they had Jason Steele's address and headed there. When they arrived at Henley Manor, they came to a large closed gate with a telephone at the side. The telephone connected to the house and was answered by a male voice asking how he could help. Petro replied I would like to talk to Jason Steele about his battery project and was told that Jason was in a meeting but should be back within the hour if he would like to come to the manor house and wait. Petro agreed and the gates swung open.

Jason, we have a problem came the telepathic message from Anita. What's happened responded Jason. There are six armed men in the house wanting to talk to you. I haven't tried to do anything physical with them as I'm worried for David, but you better come home as soon as possible. Jason replied he would be there in 15 minutes.

When Jason arrived home, he immediately recognised Petro, although it took a few minutes for Petro to recognise him as Doctor Hussein. "Petro, I realise you have problems and I'd like the two of us to go into my office where I'll give you a full explanation" said Jason, to which Petro agreed.

Jason then went into a detailed explanation of how he was a member of Britain's MI6 and the service had been watching both Petro and Khalifa's operation for a considerable time period. Al Qaeda had been their initial target and sophisticated listening devices picked up the initial contact from them to your organization for the purchase of the six nuclear weapons. We found out that Al Qaeda planned on detonating the nuclear weapons in four major cities in the USA as well as London and Manchester in the UK. Although we weren't too concerned when the weapons were under your control, as soon as we realised Al Qaeda were closing in on getting their purchase price, we had to take action. We knew where you were storing the weapons and we had a team go to your site to recover them. We used a newly developed sleeping gas to disable your sentries and I went in to supervise the weapons removal. I thought we had taken care of the security cameras, but our technical guy must have messed up by leaving me on there for you to find.

My boss in MI6 originally wanted to arrest Khalifa and his followers and let the Russian authorities deal with your group. We have been trying to capture Ayman, but he and his senior advisors are too heavily guarded in Pakistan and Afghanistan and our efforts haven't been successful. However, we would like you to help us in this effort and if you provide the assistance we need, we will ensure that you receive one billion pounds in diamonds. This is only half the amount you were to receive from Al Qaeda, but as you no longer have the nuclear weapons if you decide not to help us you will have no money. Either way we are no longer interested in prosecuting you for the original weapons theft.

Petro knew that a billion pounds would be more than sufficient to give each of his team an amount they would be able to live comfortably on for the rest of their lives. So, he agreed with Jason and asked him what was required from his group. Jason said the first thing is to tell Khalifa they had made a mistake about the weapons, which had been moved to a different storage area without his knowledge. Let him know the soldiers responsible for moving the weapons had been disciplined. Next, he should contact Ayman and ask if he could have one of his experts check the diamonds they had acquired currently as the sale was getting so close. Jason said that he would disguise himself as a Dutch diamond dealer and accompany him when Ayman agreed to the meeting. Although Petro's men did not have any Muslims in their membership, it was important that they should also be convinced they still had control over the weapons. He could tell them whatever tale he needed to, but if Ayman has any reason to believe they had lost control of the weapons, the deal was off. Jason also asked Petro how he had been able to acquire the sophisticated handguns he and his men had. Petro explained that Ayman had arranged for that with his contact, the Imam of the central mosque. Yes, I think I met him, said Jason, is that Ahmed Hussain? When Petro responded in the affirmative Jason knew there was yet one more problem he would have to resolve. Where on earth do they keep such weapons asked Jason, and Petro told him how the Imam had walked him downstairs in the mosque to a very well stocked armoury.

Petro reluctantly agreed with Jason and they shook hands on the deal. Returning to the living room, Petro told his men that everything had been resolved and they would be heading back to the Ukraine the following day. Thanking David and Anita for their hospitality, Petro and his men left the house and returned to their hotel. That evening Petro returned the guns and ammunition to Ahmed Hussein and told him that there had been a mix up and the problem they anticipated failed to materialise. He also asked Ahmed to thank Ayman for his assistance and tell him the trip to London was due to a misunderstanding and they no longer had a problem.

20

LONDON, FEBRUARY 2016

Jason was invited again for dinner with Richard at his club. Once they were settled in another of the many private rooms in White's, Jason updated Richard on the weapons status over a pre-dinner drink. Although Richard wasn't happy about giving the Ukrainians' so much money, Jason said he needed their assistance for his plan to work. Telling Richard, he would be travelling to Amsterdam to visit one of their many diamond factories, Jason discussed how he planned on getting to Ayman's hiding place for the diamonds they already possessed. I plan on taking a crash course in the Dutch language as well as diamonds and their values. I do know that there are five carats in a gram, and a one carat diamond is worth between 7 and 8 thousand US dollars. So, one billion dollars' worth of diamonds would probably weigh around sixty pounds. A lot depends on the individual size and quality of the diamonds and I am hoping I'll be able to be able to assess the stones values after spending time with an expert.

Jason then explained how his meeting with Petro had been very successful and that Petro had agreed to accompany him on a trip to see Ayman Mohammed and value the diamonds. Although he was uncertain how he would be able to infiltrate Ayman's security devices, he intended to take all the diamonds and after giving Petro his share, return the balance to help MI6 funding. Although Richard had no idea how Jason would be able to get hold of the diamonds, he agreed with Jason's plans and wished him good luck. "One last item," said Jason, "Petro visited me with five of his group. They were all armed with new Glock 17's and when I asked him how they were acquired, he explained that Ayman Mohammed arranged for him to pick up weapons from Ahmed Hussain, the Imam of the Central mosque. He told me how the Imam took him downstairs in the mosque and how he arrived at an area with several doors, one of which was the storage area for a well-stocked arsenal of weapons. I do not know how you would obtain a search warrant, but I strongly suggest you raid the mosque and remove all the weapons there. If you like, I am prepared to put on the Suleiman Hussein disguise and accompany you to the Magistrates Court as a witness to the arms stored there." Richard asked Jason to leave that with him and he would discuss the issue with his MI5 counterpart who were technically responsible for counterintelligence in the UK.

Arriving home after the fruitful meeting with Richard, Jason joined Anita and David in the living room where they were enjoying an after-dinner drink and discussing Jason's involvement with the Saudis and

Ukrainians. "I think I'll join you two and bring you up to date on our recent visitors," said Jason. He then went on to explain how he was working on an undercover operation for MI6 to prevent an act of terrorism in the UK. Although the work isn't dangerous, I have been asked by our neighbour, Richard James, to keep my involvement confidential. In fact, I have an interesting assignment tomorrow when I must travel to Amsterdam for a couple of days to do some research on the diamond industry. I thought the trip would make a nice break for you Anita, if dad doesn't mind being left alone again." "Certainly not," said David. He explained that he was very busy trying to source a supply for the additional equipment Jason had asked for to further his battery development and it would be nice to have some peace and quiet.

21

AMSTERDAM, FEBRUARY 2016

The KLM flight to Amsterdam landed on time, and Jason lost no time in getting a taxi to the Gassan diamond factory in Nieuwe Ullenburgerstraat. Anita had expressed an interest in learning about diamonds as well, so agreed to join him on the factory trip. She also added the check in time at the hotel was 4pm anyway, and she would much rather spend the time with Jason at Gassans. During the flight Jason explained that Amsterdam had a long history in the diamond trade dating back to when the Sephardic Jews introduced the diamond cutting industry in the 16th century. The hour long tour he booked when he was in London consisted of a visit to the diamond factory to see the transformation of a rough diamond into a dazzling brilliant followed by a visit to the showrooms where experts would explain the various sizes and qualities of the diamonds. Arriving at the factory after a 25-minute taxi drive, Jason asked the taxi driver to wait for them while they took the one-hour factory tour, and then take them to the Waldorf Astoria hotel where they had booked a suite for two nights. Entering the factory Jason was met by a charming young lady who introduced herself as Catherina. As he had booked a tour for just the two of them, Catherina explained that she would be conducting the tour and asked them what they hoped to achieve on the visit. Jason explained his main interest was in being able to tell the value of a diamond as he was in the market for an expensive diamond ring, and he did not want to buy an inferior stone.

After congratulating Anita on having such a considerate husband, Catherina told Jason she would do her best to explain how the grading process worked and that the four main components contributing to its value are the diamond's colour, clarity, cut and carat. They went firstly to the factory where they watched a craftsman cutting a diamond. She explained there were two types of meanings to diamond cuts, and the first relates to the actual shape of the finished diamond. Our craftsman is cutting the stone you see into an oval shape, but there are many other shapes such as round, heart, marquise, pear etc. depending on the buyer's specifications. She added that the popularity of different shapes depends on current trends, but that rounds are always in great demand. However, round cuts result in the greatest waste of diamond rough but with their greater value, the waste is often ignored.

The second relates to the specific quality of cut for the shape, and that will determine the quality and price of the product. This is the stage where our craftsman fashions the stone so that its proportions and symmetry deliver a stone that interacts with light to provide the best possible visual effects. The length of the stone from top to bottom (culet to bottom of the girdle) is called the pavilion depth, and if that depth is too deep or too shallow, light can escape from the sides which will reduce the diamond's value. Another important factor with a diamond is its clarity. As diamonds are the result of carbon being exposed to tremendous heat and pressure deep in the earth, they can end up with numerous internal (inclusions) and external (blemishes) characteristics that influence the price. There is a diamond clarity scale that has six major categories, but at the top of the scale is Flawless (FL) which has no visible inclusions or blemishes. Many inclusions and blemishes are too small to be visible to the naked eye, which is why a trained diamond grader will view the diamond using a small magnifying glass called a loupe to determine its clarity.

Explaining a diamond's colour, Catherina said that pure diamonds are perfectly transparent and colourless. However, they do occur in several colours including white, red, green, yellow and even black. Pricing has four basic ranges:

Relatively affordable range: Which includes grey, brown and fancy yellow diamonds.

Mid-range: Which includes intense and vivid yellow diamonds and orange diamonds.

High Price range: Which include pink, purple, violet, green and blue diamonds.

Ultra-High range: The rarest diamond colour and the most expensive is red.

Finally, Catherina explained about the diamond sizes which are measured in carats. Here as larger carat diamonds are rarer than smaller, the prices are more than double the weight differences. For example, a 1 carat diamond could cost between $1,300 and $16,500 depending on the previously discussed cut quality, clarity, colour and shape. However, a 2-carat diamond with the same attributes as the 1 carat diamond would cost between $5,000 and $60,000. When Jason asked what a 2.5 diamond carat would cost, Catherina's answer was between $10,000 for a low-quality diamond to upwards of $100,000 for a best quality diamond. Thanking Catherina for her detailed explanations, Jason asked her if it would be possible to get any reports on the grading process. Catherina said she would be glad to provide him with a copy of the GIA diamond grading report which included an assessment of the colour, clarity, cut and carat weight with a diagram of clarity characteristics and a graphic representation of the diamond's proportions. When asked if the report was prepared in Holland, Catherina explained it was produced by the Gemological Institute of America who are the world's foremost authority on diamonds.

Declining Catherina's suggestion of a visit to the diamond showrooms with a promise to return at a later date after studying the grading report, Jason and Anita returned to their taxi with a copy of the report and headed to the hotel.

The Waldorf Astoria is on Amsterdam's Herengracht canal and has been converted from six 17th and 18th century palaces to its current 93 rooms and suites. Anita had booked them into a King Grand Junior Suite which had a view over the canal. Anita decided she would take a stroll around the area after Jason told her he would like to listen to the Dutch language course he purchased as part of the Rosetta Stone package he purchased in London. Although the lessons were 10 minutes long, Jason fast forwarded some of the content and had a good working knowledge of the language by dinner time. After talking to Anita, they decided to try the Librije's Zusje restaurant in the hotel which boasted a two Michelin star chef. The restaurant was recommended by the concierge who explained the head chef recently returned from Hong Kong where he was the Executive Chef of the Landmark Mandarin Hotel. They enjoyed a very pleasant and leisurely meal, and enjoyed several conversations talking to the staff in Dutch. The hotel had booked a private Dutch tutor for the following day, and Anita decided she would like to join in the lesson. Listening to Jason's tapes after dinner, Anita was amazed at how easy the language appeared and was looking forward to talking with a native Dutch speaker the next day. The tutor was suitably impressed with both of their language capabilities after the class, and even wondered if they were also Dutch nationals who had been sent to assess his teaching skills. Heading back to London the next morning, Jason reviewed the GIA reports on the flight and by the time he reached London was more than satisfied with the results of the trip.

22

LONDON, FEBRUARY 2016

Jason sat down with Anita and went over his plans for relieving Al Qaeda of their diamond collection. Having memorised the GIA reports, he felt confident of being able to put a value to the diamond collection. He was also certain that Petro would help as much as he could. Petro was not happy to learn about Ayman's plans for setting the six warheads off in the USA and the UK and was concerned about Al Qaeda's plans to kill as many non-Muslim's as possible. Jason's biggest worry was could Petro convince Ayman of his need to check the diamonds they currently held. That would mean Jason having to travel with Petro to possibly Afghanistan which was an extremely dangerous country for a Westerner. Jason reassured Anita that if things got bad, he could always transport himself back home, and said he would also take Petro with him. The only reason for the trip was to see where the diamonds were being held so he could return later and move the diamonds to London. Although she was concerned, Anita told Jason she considered the trip was essential as that much money in the hands of terrorists would only end with an alternative method of killing innocent people.

So, Jason called Petro and asked him to set up a meeting with Ayman and introduce Jason as a Dutch diamond expert he wanted to examine the diamonds to ensure their quality before releasing the nuclear weapons. Petro decided to call Khalifa to put his request in as Ayman was very concerned about Western agents being able to monitor his telephone calls. Khalifa went through numerous people using code names to eventually get the message to Ayman. The response came back that although Ayman was not happy about being questioned on his word concerning the diamonds value, he agreed to meet with Petro and his expert. It would have to be at one of his locations in Afghanistan and he needed to know the Dutch expert's name. Jason decided on the name Jacob Eckhardt and asked Richard if he could arrange for a Dutch passport in that name as well as fabricating a background in the diamond industry in case Ayman decided to check up on him.

Since finding how easy he found learning languages, Jason had set a target of learning a new language every day. However, he was unfamiliar with most of the languages spoken in Afghanistan. Having mastered the 24 languages in the Rosetta Stone courses he was fluent in their Persian course, which was Farsi, the language spoken in Iran. About half of the Afghans speak a version of Farsi with the most popular being Dari, but many other dialects are spoken including Tajik and Hazara. Many Afghans speak Pashto, the language of the Pashtuns and Jason decided he needed to see if Richard had any Afghans working in MI6 he could use to learn as much of the local dialects as possible before his trip.

Richard was able to find two native Afghan speakers and arranged for Jason to spend as much time with them as he liked. He also said it would take a few days to get the passport from the Dutch embassy, but Jason said that would not be a problem as he did not expect the trip to take place for at least two weeks.

Jason wondered where Ayman's hideout would be and thought he may have gone to Bin Laden's old hideout of Tora Bora as Al Qaeda still had a presence there. When the Americans tried to capture Bin Laden in 2001, Bin Laden and many other Al Qaeda leaders escaped from Tora Bora to Pakistan, where Bin Laden was finally killed nearly ten years later. Although the US tried to free Tora Bora from Al Qaeda, they had not been successful so Ayman could well be hiding in the cave complex. If they had to travel to Tora Bora, it would be the most dangerous trip Jason had ever encountered.

Jason met up with his two Afghan speakers for two days. Abdul Baqi was the lead instructor and when Jason told him about his planned trip to Tora Bora, he strongly advised against making such a trip because of the dangers from the various factions in the region. When Jason said he had to make the trip, and that he would be meeting with Taliban leaders, Abdul told him that although most people in Afghanistan spoke Dari which is the Taliban's preferred language, Pashto was also understood by many and in Kabul where Abdul was raised people spoke and understood Hindustani due to the popularity of Bollywood films. Jason spoke to Abdul in the Iranian Farsi he had studied, and Abdul was amazed at his proficiency in the language. "I think we will be able to teach you a number of the different dialects over the next two days" said Abdul. At the end of the intensive course, Jason was able to speak with a local accent in Dari, Pashto, Uzbek and Turkmen, and planned on listening to his tapes on Hindustani before the trip.

23

LONDON, MARCH 2016

Jason received a call from Petro to say that Khalifa would meet with them at the border between Afghan and Iran and escort them to Ayman in two weeks' time. Petro had contacts in Istanbul, and they would supply him with a six-seater 4x4 plus guns and ammunition that may be required. Explaining the trip, Petro said he would be accompanied by three of his men and taking turns in driving, they would leave Tehran early morning and drive to Torbat E Jam where they would spend the night, then meet up with Ayman's men at the Islam Qala border crossing. The Taliban would ensure they had a safe journey from there to Ayman's safe house which was on the outskirts of Kabul. They would all be able to obtain visas for Afghanistan at the border crossing. On asking why they could not just fly into Kabul, Petro responded his Iranian contacts were better than his Afghan contacts, but that if Jason preferred to fly to Kabul, he would be picked up there. Jason said with his time constraints he would prefer to fly to Kabul, so they agreed to meet up at the Kabul airport in 16 days' time.

Calling Richard later that day, Jason updated him on the plans for his trip to Afghanistan. He explained that Petro wanted to get there by driving from Istanbul where he had good military contacts, but it would be fine for him to meet Petro at the Kabul airport. In addition to the Dutch passport, Jason asked him to get a visa for Afghanistan for him. Richard said they were in the process of adding immigration stamps to various countries on the passport which had an issue date in 2010. They had established a new identity for Jacob Eckhardt including school certificates, work references plus setting up a small office for him with one secretary and business cards for the Eckhardt Fine Jewellery Company established in 2012. The work references were from two Dutch diamond companies who had helped MI6 on several occasions. He agreed to obtain the visa for Afghanistan and expected to have the passport to him well before his travel date. Although Richard tried to get Jason to give him details of how he expected to obtain the diamonds from an obviously well-guarded location, Jason told him the contacts he had demanded complete privacy and that even he did not know how they were going to accomplish the task. All they have asked for is the location of the diamonds and a 5% fee for delivering them to him in London.

Sitting down with Anita that evening, Jason explained how the Afghanistan trip would be the last step in stopping the immediate Al Qaeda threat, although it was very difficult to see a long-term solution. Anita agreed the situation was complex, but in her view, nothing could be changed permanently unless the Afghan government continued working to improve education standards, in particular for women. It will take many years before significant changes are made, but it can be done, and we only have to look at our own history to see how the West has changed in their acceptance of women as equal partners. "It's a pity you couldn't come on the trip if it had started in Istanbul, as you could see how advanced things there in comparison to Saudi Arabia are," said Jason. "Once this is all over, we will have to spend a week or so travelling in Turkey"

24

KABUL, APRIL 2016

"I don't understand why you couldn't explain things over the telephone Khalifa" said Ayman Mohammed at the Kabul airport. Khalifa had called Ayman the previous day and asked him to meet him at the airport on urgent business. "I think we have a serious problem, but I really don't understand it." said Khalifa. Then Khalifa went on to remind Ayman how Petro had arrived in London, questioned his nephew Mohamed about the missing weapons, found out that Doctor Suleiman Hussein was really Jason Steele who employed Mohamed in research for his company, and after talking to this Steele person came back to me and said the missing weapons were not in fact missing. "I remembered that Mohamed requested a picture of a person called Jason Steele who I met in Saudi. I had another nephew named Sabah who dishonoured the family name by marrying a Western woman he met in University. Years later Sabah and his woman returned to Saudi, and Sabah went to work for

SOCO in Dammam. I had planned a military exercise to take over a housing complex in Al Khobar, where some very senior SOCO employees, high ranking Saudi's including princes, and Foreign diplomats were attending a dinner function. My plan was to force the Saudi authorities into releasing one of my sons and two of his cousins in exchange for the many people I held in captivity. I was surprised to recognize one of the captives as Sabah with whom I assumed to be his British woman. When Sabah offered some resistance, I took the opportunity to perform an honour killing to remove Sabah from the family. I thought I had also executed his woman, but she survived, and then went on to return to the UK and marry this Jason Steele. When I met Suleiman Hussein, I did not recognise him as Jason Steele, but after Mohamed told us he really was, I thought back to one of the captives I met in Saudi and realized there were a lot of similarities.

Over the next few weeks, I kept asking myself if there was any connection between Mohamed's comment that the nuclear weapons should be checked and the trip by whom I thought was his Saudi Physics professor. I was convinced that Suleiman was who he claimed to be, and his membership in the mosque and apparent dislike of foreigners working in Saudi equalled my own. However, when Petro asked me to contact you to arrange the meeting with his Dutch diamond expert to check the quality of the diamonds, I couldn't help but think how similar that was to the request to check the nuclear weapons. I decided that as I remembered the photograph of Jason Steele and probably met him in Saudi, I should come to Kabul to see if there is any resemblance to the Dutch diamond expert. I'm probably being over cautious, but this deal is far too important for us to run into problems." Ayman thanked Khalifa for his commitment to the project and welcomed his addition to the Kabul team. He told Khalifa that in addition to the diamond expert and Petro, there would also be three of Petro's men in the group. Khalifa ended the conversation by saying "I almost forgot to mention the problem we had at the London mosque shortly after Petro's visit. It was raided by the police who arrived with a search warrant, and the Imam has been arrested after they found the armoury in the basement. Could be a coincidence, but just another unexpected set back."

It was a tiring flight for Jason. Setting off in the early afternoon, he had booked on Emirates Airlines for a seven-hour flight from London to Dubai, then a four-hour layover in Dubai followed by a three-hour flight to Kabul. On leaving immigration, Jason was glad to see Petro in the waiting area. Walking up to Petro, it took him a while to convince Petro who he was. Jason thought if Petro was taken by surprise, he should be fine with Khalifa and Ayman. Petro explained that his group arrived yesterday and were already booked into the Kabul Serana Hotel which is situated in the centre of Kabul and only a twenty-minute drive from the airport. After collecting his suitcase Jason was taken to the hotel and Petro commented on how the hotel's security is first class so we should be very safe in staying there. "I booked you in for two nights" said Petro, "as I knew your flight arrived in the early morning. You can get some sleep and we will meet up at 2pm in reception. We have our car and will follow Ayman's driver to their housing compound."

After checking in, Jason went to his room which was larger than expected, but as soon as he unpacked his case, he locked the hotel room door and transported himself home. Anita was surprised to see him, but he said I was a bit tired and thought that even though I'm in a nice room in a hotel in Kabul, why not take advantage of our fantastic travel capability. So, Jason had a sleep in his own bed, shaved and showered then transported himself back to the hotel just before 2 pm. With his diamond colorimeter, calibrated scales and jeweller's Eye Loupe in his briefcase, Jason headed down to reception and met up with Petro. Saying hi to Borys and Petro's two other men, the five went to their car which was a new Audi Q7 seven-seater. Petro explained to Jason that they would meet Ayman's driver after leaving the Green Zone, which is a heavily fortified and walled off compound where some of the best protection in Kabul can be found. On passing guards at one of the entry points, Petro received a telephone call and drove for a few kilometres before reaching a petrol station. There were two vehicles parked at the petrol station, a Toyota Corolla and a Toyota Land Cruiser. Petro went to the Corolla and spoke to the driver who appeared to be an Afghani. After pointing to the Land Cruiser, the driver wound his window up and Petro came back to the SUV. "We are to follow the Corolla and the Land Cruiser will follow us for security purposes. We will travel West for about twenty kilometres before we reach Ayman's compound."

"They have just arrived at the compound", Ayman told Khalifa. "I will take their expert to see the diamonds and once they have finished bring them here to meet you. If you recognise the man as Jason Steele, we will detain them and get to the bottom of whatever they are trying to do." Ayman left Khalifa in his house and walked to the compound gates. He had a security detail of four heavily armed Al Qaeda Mujahideen manning the gates 24 hours a day. They had their own accommodation in the compound and operated in 8-hour shifts. In addition to the guards, there were a dozen of his senior fighters also based in the compound, which had a total of eight buildings. The building where the diamonds were stored had two armed Mujahideen on duty outside the building as well as two more inside the building. The diamonds were stored in a prefabricated strong room made from stainless steel with a two key plus digital keypad to open the strong room door, followed by a second door with stainless steel bars and a biometric door lock that only Ayman and his two deputies could enter. Ayman instructed the gate guards to allow access for the visitors and had them park in the area by the security office.

Arriving at the walled compound, Jason was impressed by the security in place. Petro spoke to a very well-armed guard at the steel entry gate and received approval to enter the compound and park in a visitor's parking area. After a few minutes, another heavily armed guard appeared from one of the villas and walked to them. "Please follow me and I will take you to Mr. Ayman" the guard said to Petro. "Mr. Ayman requests you only bring your diamond consultant and for the rest of your group to remain in the vehicle. Also, you must leave any weapons in the vehicle." Petro asked his men to stay alert and told Jason to follow him.

Walking through the compound which seemed very well maintained with lawns and trees but no animals or children playing, they approached the only building with outside guards. Ayman and one of his senior men were standing at the entry talking to the guards and greeted Petro and Jason as they arrived. Entering the building, they were in a large reception area with several closed wooden doors leading to parts of the building plus a very large steel door that Ayman and his companion approached, each holding a key. After Ayman entered some numbers on a keypad, he and his associate placed their keys into locks and slowly opened the door. Ayman explained to Petro and Jason that the actual vault was a sealed unit, and they had safety measures in place to ensure the door was never closed with somebody inside. There was a second door made up from steel bars in a frame and Ayman approached the door handle which had a small scanner above it. Ayman said they had installed additional security in the form of an iris scanner and he was one of only three people that could get through this door. Once inside the room, there were several storage cabinets and Ayman explained to Jason the diamonds were stored in trays in the cabinets according to colour and carat size which were clearly marked. There was a table in the room as well as two chairs, and Ayman said he would leave his assistant with Jason during Jason's examination of the diamonds while he would accompany Petro to their guest villa for refreshments.

Jason started his appraisal at an end cabinet which had a sign in English saying "Coloured diamonds. When he saw the different colours, he noticed one tray marked "Red". Looking at the tray he saw many small red diamonds but there were also several diamonds marked as 1 carat and above. Checking the largest diamond, he found that it was a perfect red diamond weighing 1.71 carats. Remembering his valuations training from Amsterdam, he knew that a 1 carat red diamond was worth at least $US 1 million and that the largest known red diamond, the Moussaieff, was a 5.11 carat diamond valued at over $20 million. Jason entered a conservative value of $US 30 million into his laptop for the value of the tray of red diamonds. The trays were sorted by colours and the rarest were the pink, purple, green, violet, pure orange and blue diamonds, followed by trays of lesser valued colours. Entering the values by colour and totalling them he arrived at a total value of $US 750 million. There remained a further 19 cabinets of clear diamonds, again sorted by carats. Jason knew the largest cut diamond, the Star of Africa 1, also known as the Cullinan, was 530 carats and worth around $US 400 million. The largest clear diamonds in the cabinets were in the 10 carat and above range, with several cabinets of below 1 carat diamonds. Once Jason had finished checking all the cabinets, he had a rough valuation of $US 1.5 billion.

Telling the assistant he was finished with his inspection, Jason was led to the main house and shown into a large reception room where Petro and Ayman were seated around a table drinking coffee with two other people. Jason immediately recognised Khalifa and hoped his disguise would be good enough to ensure he wasn't recognized. "I hope you were satisfied with our diamond collection Mr. Eckhardt," said Ayman. "Yes, very impressed" replied Jason, "and I'm also impressed by the way you have them stored so professionally." "I'd like to introduce you to Mr, Gerard De Groot," said Ayman. "Gerard has been working for us for several years and previously was employed in the diamond industry. He has been responsible for selecting and purchasing all the diamonds in our collection." "Goedenmiddag" said Mr. De Groot in Dutch and proceeded to speak to Jason in rapid fire Dutch, asking him how long he had been working in the diamond industry as it was strange he didn't recognize him from his Amsterdam contacts. Jason had his story ready and was glad that Richard had fabricated a Dutch nationality for him but had him working for De Beers in Botswana before moving to their Luxembourg head office in 2000 and then helping establish their New York operation in 2005.

"Excuse us for talking in our native tongue" said Jason, "but it's so nice to meet a fellow Dutchman." After introducing Khalifa as a member of his organization, Ayman insisted on Jason having a coffee while he walked Mr. De Groot who had an urgent meeting to the gate. On leaving the house, Ayman asked Gerard what his opinion of Mr. Eckhardt was. He replied that he was definitely a Dutchman and he had retained his Dutch accent even though he worked in different countries. Ayman thanked Gerard and returned to his house. Taking Khalifa to his office, he asked him if

Eckhardt was really Jason Steele. Khalifa said he didn't think so. Eckhardt was older than Steele, had different colouring including hair and eyes, and his voice was completely different to Steele. Ayman returned to Petro and Jason and asked Petro if there was any other business to be conducted. When Petro said he was happy with their visit and expected Ayman to obtain the rest of the diamonds in the not-too-distant future at which time they would release the warheads, Petro and Jason took their leave from Ayman and returned to their vehicle. Ayman had arranged for his men to lead Petro back to the entrance of the Green Zone to ensure they would be safe en-route.

"I'm glad to hear they have the value of diamonds they have been telling us," said Petro. "However, I don't see any way your contacts will be able to get the diamonds with all the security Ayman has." When Jason admitted he did not know how it could be accomplished either, the group set off on their return trip. Although Jason had the capability to transport himself home, he decided to take the flight from Kabul in case Ayman had people watching him. Returning to their hotel at 6pm, Jason agreed to meet up with Petro and his men at 8pm for dinner at the hotel's Silk Route Restaurant. Heading to his room, Jason decided to transport himself home to bring Anita up to speed om his visit. He told her that Ayman had brought Khalifa to the meeting, but his disguise had fooled him when he read Khalifa's mind and knew he was going to report that he was not Jason Steele to Ayman. He also explained how he needed to fly back to London and that his flight from Kabul did not leave until 4pm the following day. As there was a seven hour wait in Dubai for his connecting flight, he would not arrive in London until 7am in two days time. After a quick shower and change of clothes, Jason sat down with Anita and they enjoyed a glass of wine before Jason headed back to Kabul.

Meeting up with Petro and group at the restaurant, Jason was impressed with the friendliness and service of the restaurant staff and enjoyed a very nice poached salmon dinner with the surprising arrival of bottles of wine for the group. It was so strange to be sitting at a dining room in a magnificent room eating a very nice meal when the majority of the Afghan people were living in poverty. Petro and group seemed very subdued and when Jason asked if there were any problems, Petro admitted they were very disturbed by the security Ayman had at his compound and didn't see how Jason's associates would be able to obtain the diamonds. In addition, if they did manage to get the diamonds, blame would fall on him. In particular, he was worried about repercussions from all the Islamic extremists that appeared to be involved in financing the purchase of the weapons when they realised there would be no weapons. Jason assured Petro that his contacts were aware of the security Ayman had but promised him they would be able to retrieve the diamonds for him. They really wanted to be sure the diamonds were in fact there and worth what they were supposed to be. However, I suggest that when you do get the diamonds you distribute them amongst your men and tell them not to change their lifestyles for as long as it takes for the terrorists to accept their losses. I also suggest that once you have the diamonds you contact Khalifa and tell him that once again the weapons have vanished and that all attempts to find how it happened had failed. You could also tell them you had contacts in the Russian military who told him in confidence they had retrieved the weapons which were now in one of their nuclear storage sites.

After the meal, Jason said goodbye to the group who were leaving early the following morning for their long drive home. The hotel arranged for a limousine to the airport for Jason the following afternoon. On reaching his room, he hung the do not disturb sign on the door and as he had arranged for a late check out, asked for a call at 2 pm the following day. Transporting himself home, he sat with Anita telling her his plans for the diamonds. He did not want to do anything until he was back officially in the UK, and Petro and his men returned home. Anita asked about the storage area and Jason explained they were locked in a sealed room which may not have any oxygen. Even though they could now hold their breath for long periods, he intended to take a mini diving cylinder with him which would give him 30 minutes of oxygen. He would also need a heavy-duty flashlight as the room would be in complete darkness. He did not notice any cameras or motion detectors in the room but intended gathering the diamonds as quickly as possible and didn't think it would take him more than five minutes. It was nice to spend the night with Anita knowing that his job was almost complete, and he would be able to concentrate on his battery once again.

Transporting back to Kabul the following afternoon, Jason made the bed look as if it had been slept in and after a shower, packed his case and was ready to check out when the 2 o'clock call came. Arriving at the airport with no incidents, Jason waited in the First-Class lounge until his flight was called and arrived back in London after a lengthy trip that Jason had used to fill several pages of complicated formulas in his attempts to design his miniature battery.

25

LONDON, APRIL 2016

Jason called Richard James as soon as he arrived home and told him the plan for getting Ayman's diamond collection was well underway and the Ukrainians would receive their share of the collection in the next few days. When asked where he wanted the balance of the diamonds sent, Richard said why don't you ask your contacts to send the diamonds to you and I will arrange for them being picked up once you have them. Jason realised that Richard really didn't believe he would be able to produce the diamonds but considered bringing the diamonds to his home was probably the best choice. The following day, armed with a flashlight, sack and the breathing apparatus, Jason was ready to retrieve the diamonds. Although the breathing apparatus would probably be not required, he was concerned that the terrorists could have installed motion detectors in the diamond storage area and it wasn't out of the realms of possibility for them to have placed some type of poison gas release tied into the potential motion detectors. He wanted to do the job in one go, and after taking a deep breath transported himself to the diamond storage area. It was jet black in the storage room, but his flashlight provided enough light for him to see the storage cabinets. There didn't appear to be any motion detectors and no poisonous gas, so he very quickly filled his sack with all the diamonds and transported himself back to London.

Jason spent the next two days segregating the diamonds by his estimated values and finished with one pile he estimated at $US 1 billion and a second pile at $US 600 million, which was slightly more than the $1.5 billion that was Ayman's valuation of the collection. After transporting the diamonds to the storage area Petro had for the nuclear weapons, Jason called Petro and told him to check the storage area where his people had deposited the diamonds. Petro did that and was amazed to find the diamonds just as Jason had promised. They had maintained security on the storage area in case Ayman had any of his people spying on them, so he left the diamonds where they were. Over the following weeks Petro who had identified a diamond specialist in readiness for receipt of the diamonds used his specialist to segregate the diamonds into fifty groups of equal value. There were a total of thirty five people in Petro's group, and twenty six of them received diamonds to the value of $US 20 million each. The six team leaders received $US 40 million each, his two deputies $US 70 million each, and Petro retained $US 100 million for himself. To avoid any discontent in the group, Petro told his officers that the junior men had received $US 20 million each, but they should keep their own shares confidential. All were more than happy with the diamonds they received and agreed to split the group up and go their separate ways. Petro warned them all to avoid being crazy with the money as he was concerned that Al Qaeda may think their group was responsible for stealing the diamonds. The men all agreed to be careful and almost all of them said they would be leaving Ukraine. Petro thanked them for staying together through the years it took to get their money and again told them they had enough to live very comfortably for the rest of their lives but to be careful with strangers and never to reveal how they acquired their wealth.

Jason called Richard and told him he had the diamonds and considered their value to be in the region of $US 600 million. He told him they could be picked up from him at any time and explained the Ukrainians had been paid the agreed amount. He also asked Richard for a favour. He wanted MI6 to make a press release and say that MI6 had just completed an operation against al Qaeda which resulted in them recovering an undisclosed number of high-quality diamonds from their hidden storage area in Afghanistan. The diamonds had been acquired for the purpose of purchasing weapons to be used in attacking the West and MI6 were also successful in recovering several missiles from a former Russian country. The operation had been in place for several years and thanks to a number of highly skilled MI6 operatives, Al Qaeda attacks had been delayed for the immediate future. Richard agreed to make the announcement and Jason hoped that would stop Ayman from chasing after Petro and his men.

26
KABUL, MAY 2016

Ayman was stunned. Khalifa had travelled to Ayman's compound and told him about a small newspaper article in the UK's Daily Mail that talked about a long-term MI6 operation that recovered an undescribed number of diamonds as well as weapons from Al Qaeda and their agents. Khalifa said that could not be their operation as all the diamonds were in place last month when you visited, and we haven't been in the storage area since then. Khalifa insisted on checking the storage area, and when they opened it up the diamonds were gone. Ayman called all the guards together and they all agreed there was absolutely no way anyone had entered the building since the visitors were here, and that even if they had entered the building no one would be able to get in without the lock combinations, keys and the iris check. Khalifa commented that Petro had a similar problem with his nuclear weapons that vanished but re-appeared and they should check with him to see if he still had the weapons. Khalifa called Petro and asked him about the weapons and he said they were there when he checked last week, something he had been doing each week since their earlier problem. He promised to check them immediately and call him back. Two hours later Petro called back and said he could not understand it, but they had checked the whole storage area and the weapons had gone again. They both agreed to get experts in to check their storage areas and see if they could come up with any way MI6 could have done what they appeared to have done.

Ayman and Khalifa talked for hours about the big problem they had. They needed to tell all the groups that contributed to the purchase of the diamonds that it appeared as if the diamonds had been stolen from their secured storage area by the British MI6 group. They also had to tell their followers that the nuclear weapons they had planned to use in the US and UK had also been recovered by MI6. It appeared they would have to defer their planned attacks on the Western countries until they had obtained a new war chest, or they could discover what MI6 had done with their diamonds.

27
LONDON, MAY 2016

J ason had been in touch with Azriel telepathically and explained how he had temporarily resolved the Al Qaeda nuclear attacks, but that he had used the transportation device several times over the last few months and wondered if that would be a problem. Azriel told him that he needed to be checked out just in case, and suggested he take Anita with him and stay for a few days in Elysium. Explaining that they should transport themselves to the place where they originally arrived and explain to the receptionist that he needed to have his cells checked. The receptionist would arrange for the check up and book them a room for as long as they wanted to stay.

Sitting down with David and Anita, Jason told David that in addition to his work on the miniature battery, he had also been recruited by MI6 to provide them with his expertise gained from his time in Saudi Arabia. Having just finished an undercover operation that resulted in a large armoury being confiscated from a mosque in Central London, he was considering taking Anita away for a week's holiday if David had no objections. "Certainly not" said David," in fact it may be nicer for you to take Anita away for two weeks." Jason agreed with his dad and thought that apart from the brief trip to Holland, the last real holiday had been their shortened honeymoon and that was unbelievably over six years ago.

Later in bed, Jason said he needed to return to Elysium to get a check up after using the transportation capability far more than the recommended once monthly use. I was thinking that after the check up, we could go to one of the Elysium libraries and pick a different planet to visit. That would be fantastic said Anita, and the pair fell asleep dreaming of what adventures they would find in other planets.

Made in the USA
Middletown, DE
03 July 2021

43562148R00080